Discard
5/04

A SNAKE NAMED SAM

Westminster Press Books
by
MARY PHRANER WARREN

Walk in My Moccasins
Shadow on the Valley
Eight Bells for Wendy
A Snake Named Sam

A SNAKE
NAMED SAM

by
MARY PHRANER WARREN

Illustrated by
BETH AND JOE KRUSH

THE WESTMINSTER PRESS
Philadelphia

STANDARD BOOK No. 664–32449–5

LIBRARY OF CONGRESS CATALOG CARD No. 72–76886

BOOK DESIGN BY
DOROTHY ALDEN SMITH

PUBLISHED BY THE WESTMINSTER PRESS ®
PHILADELPHIA, PENNSYLVANIA

PRINTED IN THE UNITED STATES OF AMERICA

For Fred, Mike, and Roy, my sons,
and for Bill Warner and Mel Johnson,
who dreamed up the real school upon which the River School is based

Contents

CHAPTER 1

THE WONDERFUL FIND

A hand opened the back door. Sneaky feet crept across the kitchen and stopped.

The living room was empty!

Redheaded Corky Downs collapsed in a chair. A happy grin spread across his freckled face. School books thudded to the floor. His long arms sliced the air.

"Yippee!" he hollered. "I made it!"

The sour taste left by a miserable morning at his new school went away. A free afternoon with Nogs lay ahead! But how long would Mom stay away on her huckleberrying trip? Better not waste a minute!

Corky swooped up his books and dumped them helterskelter on the army cot in his bedroom off the kitchen. Next he hustled around filling his tackle box with sinkers and hooks.

"Ta-tee-ta," he hummed. "Lemme see . . . oh, yes!" He had promised Nogs he would bring along his terrific, stupendous, unusual pet, Sam.

"Too bad," he muttered, searching for the key to Sam's cage among the nests and fossils on the shelf. "Too bad I am the only one in this house who appreciates reptiles."

There was the key, behind a hornet's nest. Corky unlocked the big screen-wire door on his pet's cage. The cage, built of wood, glass, and screening, stood on his worktable. It was padlocked, not because Sam was dangerous, but because he was a first-class escape artist. And Sam was four feet long.

"Come, boy, in you go!" Corky dumped his orange-and-brown pet into a flour sack he used for a collecting bag. Sam did not mind this sudden change of scenery. The bag was a second home to him. When the Downs family had moved to Portland from eastern Oregon, he had traveled comfortably in its dark folds. He could go without water for several days, and plenty of air seeped through the loosely woven cloth.

Corky snapped a rubber band around the top of the bag. At the back door, he whistled like a robin. "Cheery-up, cheery-up!"

A scrawny boy with hair the color of mud dropped out of the cherry tree. He was just as short for his age as Corky was tall. He flew into the house.

"I think that old guy next door saw me, Corky!"

"Mr. Scarborough? Fat chance. He's eighty and almost blind. All he thinks of is his cats. Here, Nogs, you load this paper bag with food from under the back steps. I'll get the extra rod." Corky loped off toward the garage.

Moments later they were on their way. Nogs bounced along to keep up with Corky's long steps down the alley between the trailer court and the paper-box factory. They ducked through the backyards of a row of houses. On the other side of the highway ran the Columbia River.

Rods over their shoulders, they stood waiting at the edge of the road. A string of cars whizzed by. One truck driver honked at them.

They raced across. Corky turned to stick out his tongue.

"NIFTY SERVICE," read Nogs from the back of the disappearing truck.

"My dad has a new job with that company," Corky told him. "They haul office equipment, kitchen ranges and stuff, all over. He's out in Gresham today."

Corky wiped his freckled forehead with his knuckles. A drop of sweat trickled into his ear. "Wow! This is sure a scorcher! I'm glad we're not with those poor kids back in Puckett's classroom."

Nogs began the chant:

> "Poor Lucy Puckett
> Fell in a bucket—
> She jumped up and down
> And didn't get drowned."

He added sadly, "I wish we'd gotten Mr. Henry instead of Miss Puckett. Mr. Henry has a St. Bernard. And a dune buggy in his garage. And he knows who's going to win the World Series. Jim Mahony and Pauline Tyler say he's always right."

"We get to have him for gym class," said Corky. He slid down the bank to the shore. Nogs followed.

They sat in the weeds to catch their breath.

"Hardly seems like the same river I lived by in eastern Oregon," said Corky. "Up there the water's bluer and the sky's bigger. Only thing you can see is a wheat barge every

now and then. And the brown hills called the Horse Heavens on the Washington side. Here it's so . . . so crowded." He waved toward the roof of a building and the docks. Small boats cluttered the water.

"It's better than school," said Nogs. "I'm starved."

"Go ahead and eat. I want to fish." Corky searched for exactly the right kind of hook. He baited it with a fat night crawler and shook the bait can. "Hope we brought enough worms."

Nogs spread his shirt on the ground. On this tablecloth he set four apples, half a loaf of bread, a jar of peanut butter and a jar of jam, and a batch of soggy salted crackers.

Now Corky could see how thin and bony Nogs looked. Like a wishbone. He threw his own shirt over a bush. The

sun felt good on his back. He went down to the edge of the water and cast his line.

While he fished, Corky gazed at the colored roofs of the city of Vancouver among the trees across the river. The Vancouver Bridge was shiny in the sun.

Corky fished for a long time. Whenever he looked at his hook, his worm was still there. He was getting hotter by the minute. And hungry. And upset.

Must be the plastic bobber. Cork bobbers seemed to bring better luck. Wasn't that how he got his nickname? Corky Downs, the boy who was always collecting bits and pieces of cork for his fishline.

Corky reeled in and went to find his tackle box. Hullo! Nogs was gone. And so was most of the lunch. Corky stared

in disgust at the crackers and two leftover apples. He had
forgotten Sam! The snake must be roasting in the sun.
While Corky munched his apple, he opened the bag and
let Sam hang around his neck to get some fresh air.

"Cork-ee! Cork-ee!"

Nogs sounded excited, but he was nowhere in sight.
Puzzled, Corky climbed the bank with the snake around
his shoulders and apple in hand.

Across the road were two houses, a field, a riding stable,
and a woodsy lot thick with a tangle of bushes. But no
Nogs.

"Cork-ee!" The sound seemed to come from the bushes.
Corky ducked through the trees to have a look.

"Here!"

Corky jumped. Before his eyes, hidden by a mess of
blackberry brambles, were the remains of an old shack.
Nogs leaned out of a window opening. "Isn't this great?
Come see!"

Great? It was perfect! Who would expect to find an
empty shack here?

"I betcha some tramp hangs out here." Corky paused.
Then he joined Nogs inside the tumbledown building. The
door squeaked on rusty hinges.

"Nope. See, I found this newspaper. It's ten years old.
The vines are so thick and stickery that I guess nobody has
bothered to look inside."

Corky licked one long scratch the stickers had made on
his arm. "Say, Nogs, let's fix it up. We don't have to tell
anyone but Pauline and Jim. If I tell my parents, they'll
probably say it might be dangerous or something."

"My folks are dead," Nogs told him. "I live with my

brother, Bill. He's a garage mechanic. He doesn't have time to bother much with me." He was walking around, peering at initials carved on the door, poking a finger into cracks, rapping on walls. "We can mend the hole in the roof, dig up some furniture, have ourselves a clubhouse."

Turning, he caught sight of what was dangling around Corky's neck. "Oh—yoweeeee! Lemme out of here!" He leaped toward the door.

"It's only Sam. You *told* me to bring him." Corky held out the long brown-and-orange snake. "Feel him, Nogs, go ahead. His skin is kind of smooth and cool. You can feel his muscles ripple. His belly is pretty too. See—black and white checks."

Nogs looked nervous. With careful fingers he grasped the snake toward the tail. But when Sam flicked out his forked tongue, Nogs backed away.

"I've got to get used to him slowly. He's the first corn snake I ever met."

"You should see my hoptoad and my frogs! And Toby, my lizard, and my other stuff," said Corky. "Now that we're living in a little city house, Mom and Dad want me to get rid of most of it."

He stroked his sleek pet. "They really want me to give Sam away. They don't like him because he eats mice."

"Live ones?" Nogs was shocked.

"Pooh! You're just like everybody else. Nobody minds when one of Mr. Scarborough's cats runs around the yard with a mouse. They say, 'Good Kitty.' But what happens when poor Sam needs one for dinner? Ugh!" Corky made a wry face, copying his mother.

"He's a constrictor, you know. He paralyzes his prey

with a nip and then coils around it and suffocates it. The mouse never knows what hit it."

A light came into Corky's blue eyes. "Hey, if they do make me give away my menagerie, I could bring it here! It wouldn't be warm enough for Sam in winter—he's from the Southeast. But my hoptoad would do all right. And so would the garter snakes and the red racer!"

"We could build shelves and make sort of a museum. Pretend we're scientists!" Nogs was catching on. "Did you catch any fish? I'm getting hungry all over again."

Corky laughed. "I got skunked. Who cares? Finding this place is better than fishing. Let's start right now looking for old junk to use. I wonder who owns this woodsy spot, anyway."

"We won't hurt anything," said Nogs. "And I didn't see any No Trespassing signs."

They treasure-hunted for a long time. Corky came up with some rope that might be handy later on. Nogs found a board that would make a dandy shelf.

"Help me get it back to the shack, Cork," he puffed. "After that, I'd better head home. I've got a three-mile hike."

Corky looked at Nogs, dismayed. "Stop by my house. I'll find you something to eat along the way."

"My brother'll whip me good if he finds out I cut school," said Nogs as they walked home.

"Won't you beat him home?" asked Corky.

"Maybe yes, maybe no. Anyhow, it was worth it. That shack . . . oh, boy! Are we ever going to have fun!"

"Are we ever! Remember, don't tell anybody except Pauline and Jim. Wish I knew what time it was."

They cut through the alley and propped their poles against the Downs garage.

"Wait here." Corky tiptoed over to the porch. Three pies were cooling on the rail. He reached for one and presented it to Nogs.

"The whole pie?" Nogs looked doubtful.

"The whole pie," said Corky grandly.

He went inside. My, but Mom had a queer gleam in her eye. Could it be after four o'clock? They hadn't seen any school friends walking home.

Was it as late as five? Corky looked sideways at the clock. His face reddened until it matched his hair.

Six twenty!

His racing mind tried to dream up a good story.

"I came home after school and I—I grabbed my rod and . . ."

Steam from the warm kitchen made his mother's butterscotch hair curl on her forehead. The pucker between her eyebrows meant that she was upset.

"If you came home at three thirty to get that rod," thundered his father's voice behind him, "how come I nearly ran you down at one o'clock when you and some other lawbreaking friend were heading toward the river?"

"You? I thought you were going to be hauling a load to Gresham today!"

Corky's father, a burly man of medium height, could look big when he wanted to. He drew himself up. "The boss," he said dryly, "happens to change his mind sometimes."

"Corky, Corky," his mother said softly, "you promised there would be no more hooky-playing when you started a new school."

"Cutting school isn't a major crime," his father said. "But hereafter, son, don't make promises you don't intend to keep."

Corky could see the hurt in the gray eyes. He was miserable.

"Dinner is over," his father said. "Make yourself a sandwich. There'll be pie when it cools."

Corky remembered the pie that was missing from the rail. He swallowed hard. He could explain it to Mom later. He hoped this would be one of Bill Noggins' late nights. It would be too bad for Nogs to get strapped. Anyway, he was glad he had given his friend the whole pie!

In the bedroom Corky let Sam hang around his shoulders while he devoured his sandwich. He was really hungry. After all, Nogs had eaten most of the lunch. The peanut-butter sandwich made Corky feel better. He went out into the kitchen and made two more, one with dill pickles sliced into it and one with honey.

Corky kept thinking about the shack. He got goose bumps on his arms.

"It's the best thing that has happened to me in a long time," he told Sam.

Sam was a good snake but he could not talk back. Corky felt lonely. And restless. He wanted to call Pauline or Jim on the telephone. But Mom and Dad were in the living room watching TV. He did not want them to hear about the shack.

For once in his life, Corky could hardly wait to go to school. He got ready for bed and crawled between the covers, but it was a long time before he slept.

CHAPTER 2

CORKY TRIES SOME TRICKS

At breakfast Mom was busy. She whisked around the kitchen sponging counters. She shoved dishes in the sink to wash later. She made lists on scraps of paper.

"Mom, about that pie . . ."

"Hush now, Corky. Get through with your meal so you can straighten up your room. Oh, I was so upset over your missing school that I guess I forgot to mention Aunt Mildred's call. She'll be spending a few days with us. And you know how fussy she is! Paul, will you be sure to fix the screen in our bedroom? It's the lock. Remember, she's fearful of burglars."

Great-aunt Millie coming to visit? Today? Horrors! Corky frowned as he took a last gulp of milk. What a rotten development!

"Good old Millie!" muttered Dad with false heartiness. When this eighty-one-year-old aunt came, he had to sleep in the living room.

"It isn't the fuss she makes," he grumbled to Corky when Mom wasn't around. "It's that she ruins any sense of privacy I have. And I wish to heavens she'd give us a few days' notice!"

He leaned over and touched Corky's shoulder lightly. "Listen, son, your great-aunt will be keeping your mother in enough of a stew these next few days. I don't want her to worry about whether or not you make it to school. No more cutting, understand?"

"Yes, sir," said Corky. "But, Dad, do I have to stick around here after school? I mean—my friends and I, we're going to have a real neat club and, well, *we* want privacy too."

His father rattled the newspaper in search of the latest baseball scores. "As long as you get your work done properly," he said, "you can play wherever you please. Within reason."

"Yes, sir!" Corky dashed off to the bedroom before Dad had a chance to change his mind. As long as Mom knew about where he was and what time he would be home, he could do almost anything. He needn't fib. He could tell her he'd be down by the river in a lot near the paper-box factory.

He kicked old tennis shoes, comic books, pajamas, checkers, chessmen, and a baseball cap under the bed. Luckily, Aunt Millie was too lame to get down on her knees to look. And Mom would be far too busy.

He mopped his shelves with a spare T-shirt and threw it under the bed with the rest of the junk, pulling his red plaid bedspread as far down as it could go. While he worked, he hummed. Pauline and Jim were going to be pea green with envy when they heard about the shack.

Corky stood in the doorway of his bedroom and gave it

a last look of inspection before leaving for school. For
Pete's sake, he must have left the lock off Sam's cage last
night. He didn't have time to look for it, so he grabbed
four books and piled them on the edge of the cage to
weight the cover. Nothing made Mom crosser than finding
the cage unlocked.

"You're going to get it!" jeered a fat boy named Skip
Lacey as soon as Corky hit the school playground. "You
and Nogs. Somebody squealed. You know what? The principal's gonna call you into his office and use that giant
paddle hanging on his wall."

"Aw, go soak your head. I didn't see any paddle when I
took him a note from Miss Puckett the other day."

"It isn't in the outer office. It's in his inner, private office.
You'll see," Skip gloated. The look on his pudgy face made
Corky wonder if he was the one who had squealed. It made
him want to give Skip a black eye. He chopped the air
with clenched fists as he roamed around looking for Pauline and Jim. Instead, he met up with Nogs, who seemed
paler than usual.

"I ate the whole pie before I got home," said the shorter
boy. "Every crumb. And I got sick. But Bill never came
in until midnight. Corky, let's not invite any girls into
our club."

"Pauline's different," Corky pointed out. "She's the best
pitcher in the sixth grade. And she's won three skateboard
contests."

That very moment, Pauline tore around the corner of
the school building. Three boys were chasing her. She
tossed a football to Corky. He caught it with a grunt and

passed it to the thin, sandy-haired fellow several feet away.

"Gee, thanks!" puffed Pauline. She flicked a dark curl out of her eyes. "You two are dopes. You know what you missed? A special assembly! Mr. Mac explained the Grow Program to us. He's deciding this week for sure who's going to be in it."

"Who cares?" Corky kicked a dirt clod. He did care very much indeed. He had heard some rumors about the principal's brand-new idea of a Grow Program. It sounded better than the regular kind of studies. "Besides," he told Pauline, "I pull such bad grades I don't stand a chance of getting picked."

"Pauline," said Nogs, "down near the river we found a shack. Nobody's been in it for years. We could tell by looking at it."

"We're cooking up a club," said Corky. "You're the one girl we want to be in it."

"Honest?" asked Pauline. But the bell rang before they could tell her any more.

"I bet we do get called into Mr. Mac's office," whispered Corky to Nogs. "I didn't make up any excuse note to hand in."

Miss Puckett was busy helping a boy find some facts in the encyclopedia. She did not see the two of them sneaking into her classroom three minutes after the bell had rung.

She looked stern, with her long black hair skinned back from her face and piled on top of her head in a braid.

Corky figured he might get Nogs or Pauline to help him look up snakes in the encyclopedia during study hall. Maybe some book or pet-store man would say corn snakes liked to eat other things besides small rodents. Then he might get to keep Sam until his pet was a ripe old age!

He had heard that corn snakes could live as long as sixteen years.

He started to work it out in the back of his notebook. Sam was two now, so maybe he had fourteen years to live. Corky was twelve. In fourteen years he would be . . . Was it twenty-seven?

Skip Lacey, who had been assigned as his seatmate, leaned across the double desk and slashed a mark through Corky's twenty-seven.

"Don't you know that twelve and fourteen are twenty-six?" hissed Skip.

Corky pretended not to hear. If he could talk Nogs and Jim into making the shack a natural history museum, he wouldn't have to wait until he grew up to do some real research. The Discoverer's Club. Say, they could call themselves the D.C.s.

Reading period dragged by. He hated reading. It was no fun to stand up in front of his reading group and let classmates hear him stumble over the hard words. Social studies next, then Math.

The morning was passing without a summons to Mr. Mac's office. Corky worked hard on his math problems. He bit the eraser clean off his pencil and chewed it, pretending it was gum. He was getting off easy!

The hand of the electric wall clock said eleven ten when the principal's secretary knocked on the door. She handed Miss Puckett a note.

"Benjamin Downs." The teacher's crisp-apple voice pierced the sudden silence. She pronounced every syllable of the hated name—*Ben-ja-min.* "Mr. Mac wishes to speak to you."

Why wasn't Nogs going too? It was unfair!

Glumly, Corky followed the secretary down the hall. He found long, stringy Mr. Mac leaning back in his swivel desk chair. His hands were clasped behind his head. He looked like a combination of Abraham Lincoln and the kind of man you could make out of pipe cleaners. His eyes, set deep in his bony face, had a questioning look.

"Sit down, young man."

Corky perched on the edge of the arm chair at the side of the big rolltop desk. His cheeks got warm. He wished he could magic himself away through the thick green carpet, out of sight.

"Name Benjamin? From what I hear on the playground, most of your pals call you—er—Corky. Am I right?"

Corky nodded.

"You just moved in from out of state?"

"No, sir. From eastern Oregon. But it might as well be another state. It's so—well, so different from western Oregon."

This time it was Mr. Mac's turn to nod. "I know what you mean—the desert, the space." He looked thoughtfully out the window. "These warm September days are great for fishing. Must have had pretty fair luck while you lived on that part of the Columbia. I've fished there myself."

Corky looked surprised.

"I like to fish," Mr. Mac told him. "I grew up here in Portland, but I know the state by heart. The rivers and streams . . . but deep-sea fishing, ah, that's what I like best! Mr. Henry and I sometimes go out in his boat and . . ."

The principal paused. "What else do you like to do, Corky?"

"Oh, I used to like to explore the desert. Hunt for lizards and snakes. I've still got quite a collection. I like to fly kites and hike. Like to play chess."

"Chess? Me too!"

The principal uncurled his pipe-cleaner body. The drawer of the desk shot open. Out came a chessboard and a box of men.

They played.

Mr. Mac took three of Corky's pawns. Corky took the principal's knight. In the end he checkmated Mr. Mac.

"You're a fine player. Now that I'm getting warmed up, let's have another go at it."

They played two more games. Mr. Mac won both. He talked in spurts—about the Grow Program and the interesting trips and projects he had in mind for those who would take part.

"The letters of the word 'Grow' stand for Growth, Research, Organization, and Work," he told Corky. "The students who are not in the program will be included in some of the best field trips. Fossil hunts. Several days at the ice caves near Bend."

"Count me out," Corky mumbled. "I flunk nearly everything."

"Who says I'm picking only top students? Some already on my list are bright. Others have gotten low grades. It doesn't mean they're dumb. Why, I brought home one sixth-grade card myself that was nothing but D's and F's!" Mr. Mac chuckled softly.

"You did?" asked Corky.

"That was the most boring year of school I ever had." Mr. Mac leaned forward, elbows on the desk, long fingers locked together. "There's more to learning than reading and memorizing facts."

He looked at Corky. "The fidgety ones and the bored ones will be invited to be in the program too."

Corky left the office in a daze. Not until he reached the door of the lunchroom did he realize that the principal hadn't said a word about his cutting school!

The Grow Program did sound like fun. If the teachers were going to choose restless students, class troublemakers, he had a chance of getting on the list!

Inside the cafeteria, he picked Nogs's worried face out of the crowd.

"Did he paddle you?" asked Nogs.

"Did he yak at you the whole time?" asked Jim.

"No," said Corky. "He didn't paddle and he didn't yak. We played chess. I won one game and he won two."

"*Chess!*" Skip Lacey choked on his tomato soup.

"That's what I said—chess." Corky saw that they couldn't believe it. He decided not to share his ideas about getting into Grow. But before the afternoon session began, he broke down and told just Nogs.

During the first period after lunch he propped his largest textbook so that Miss Lucy Puckett could not see what he was doing. Then he began to manufacture a supply of spitballs. Out of the corner of his eye, he could detect Nogs doing the same thing.

As soon as the teacher's head turned toward the chalkboard . . . *Splat!* A spitball hit Carla Rumple in the elbow. Splat! Splat! Splat!

28

A really wet one landed on the top of Roy's English paper. There! And one for Skip Lacey in the eye! It came from Nogs's side of the room when Skip was returning to his seat after writing his spelling words on the board.

The class tittered. Now Skip kept his eyes open in all directions. Corky shot a warning wink at Nogs. He slid the rest of his spitballs into his desk to save for later.

Two spots of color glowed on Miss Puckett's high cheek-bones. Had she seen the flying spitballs? He couldn't tell.

When Corky yawned out loud, the class tittered for the second time. Miss Puckett still refused to notice.

Corky stuck his legs out, pretending to stretch them. Nobody came along to trip over his feet. At last he got up and went over to the window to sharpen his pencil. No matter how hard he tried, he could not make enough noise to upset Miss Puckett.

Now the rest of the class was chuckling at the story the teacher had started to read out loud. Nogs had gotten interested too, the traitor! He was laughing until his eyes squeezed shut.

Corky stared out the window. The primary grades were having recess. Some children were playing tag. Others were throwing a ball. Corky had an idea.

He slipped into the hall. The clock out there said one fifty. The younger children had about ten minutes more before their bell would ring them in.

Gleefully, Corky reached up and pushed the button near the classroom door.

Clang! Clang! Clang!

Good grief! Oh, misery! He had meant to ring the recess

bell, so the primary children would come running into the school. He must have rung the fire gong by mistake!

Children and teachers poured down the hall. Big children, little children, fat children, thin children.

Shocked, Corky stood watching the mix-up he had started. But, come to think of it, it wasn't too mixed up at that! There had been a fire drill the first week of school, so both new and old pupils knew what to do. They streamed by Corky in bunches. Only a few forgot the rules and whispered.

Corky's class was coming. He flattened himself against the wall, half behind the open door. As soon as he could, he slipped in at the end of the sixth-grade line.

What would happen when the teacher and Mr. Mac found out who started the drill? Cutting school, upsetting classes—all in one week. Was it bad enough for Mr. Mac to expel him? He could see his parents' sad faces when the note came: "Your son, Benjamin . . ."

CHAPTER 3

A TRICK BACKFIRES

After school, Corky wanted to clear out as fast as he could. But a cheery voice behind him piped up, "Come on, let's go show the shack to Pauline and Jim."

"Can't," muttered Corky. "I forgot this was the day my aunt's coming from Idaho." He jogged off, leaving a puzzled Nogs to stare after him.

At home there was no chance to go to his room and be alone. Aunt Mildred had arrived on an early train.

"My suitcases are by the front door for you to carry upstairs. And, Benjamin, please run down to the drugstore to get some of my special cough syrup. I'll jot the name on this pad. You're looking a bit pale, Mabel." At this point she grasped Mrs. Downs's chin in her fingers and gazed into her eyes. "Benjamin, before you go, I believe your mother mentioned an extra pillow in the basement closet."

Corky's head swam with orders. His mind blotted out his snowy-headed, double-chinned Aunt Mildred. Instead, he pictured Nogs and Jim and Pauline crowded into the little gray shack making plans.

"Yes, Aunt Mildred. No, Aunt Mildred. Certainly, Aunt Mildred." He ran around doing the old lady's errands while she sipped her third cup of tea from one of Mom's beautiful yellow china teacups.

It took the best china, the best bed, the best everything, to please Aunt Mildred. Still, Mom looked strained, as if the best might not be good enough.

The suitcases were heavy. They probably held enough clothing for a whole week. Corky lugged them up the narrow stairs to Mom and Dad's bedroom. His aunt followed him, clucking, "Careful, young man, no scratches, no scratches!"

Down in the kitchen, Mom planted a kiss on his forehead. "Maybe she'll take a nap after she unpacks, and we'll have a little . . ." Her words faded into silence. From the room upstairs came a piercing shriek. Then a more deafening one, followed by a terrible wailing sound.

For one awful instant, Corky and his mother stood frozen in the middle of the kitchen floor.

"Stay where you are!" Mom ordered. "I'll go up. She may be badly hurt."

"Hurry!" begged Corky.

"Control yourself, Mildred," he could hear Mom say at the top of the stairs. "It's only Corky's snake!"

Oh, no! Corky raced into the bedroom and yanked the books from the top of Sam's cage. He reached in and lifted the flowerpot home where Sam loved to curl and sleep. No Sam!

The real mystery was the way Mom looked when she came down to the kitchen. Had she been laughing or crying? Maybe both!

"Your great-aunt Mildred is leaving on the five o'clock train," his mother announced. "I don't believe she wishes to say good-by, Corky. After I drive her to the station, you go get that snake! He's cornered between the windowpane and the screen. *Lock him into his cage!* You know what your father will say!"

Corky chewed his lower lip. "Yes, Mom. I—I guess I lost the lock. Sam must have gotten loose during the night, before I put the books on the lid of his cage."

It was going to be no more Sam when Dad got home. Dad had warned that the next time the snake got out, off he would go to the zoo.

The front door slammed. The car started. Corky took the stairs two at a clip and found his pet. "Oh, Sam!" he said sadly. "Oh, Sam! It would be warm enough to leave your cage in the shack for a while. But how would I get it there? It's too heavy to carry. I don't have a wagon. Sam, I'd like to run away with you. We could tour the country in a circus or something. Or just go live in the woods and never go to school again."

Now, more than ever, Corky wished he had a brother around to help—or at least to talk to.

He got up and put Sam in his cage. There was the lock, right on the bookshelf above the table. Why hadn't he seen it this morning? Corky snapped the lock onto the cage door and found some paper.

He scrawled a note: "Playing with Nogs and Jim on lot across from the stable."

He hurried off, hoping his friends would still be there. If they all worked quickly, they could do something about

Sam, because Mom would be caught for a while in the evening traffic downtown.

Sure enough. Jim waved from the roof of the shack where he was nailing some shingles over the holes. "Hi, Cork! This is the best!"

"Corky came after all!" squealed Pauline, looking out the window hole. "Corky, come see the stuff we hauled from our garage. Mom was so glad to get rid of it that she didn't ask any questions. I'm going to make curtains for the window in Home Ec class."

That was a girl for you, thinking of curtains! But when Corky stepped inside and saw two wobbly chairs and a table and chipped cups and saucers, all of which Pauline had brought, he forgave her.

"My dad works for a lumber company. That's how I got some shingles," said Jim, peering through the doorway. "He'll give me a piece of glass for the window if I tell him I'm making something. I know how to mix putty, too."

"We need to vote on club officers today," Pauline said briskly.

"No!" said Nogs. "That kind of club is awful. I won't stay if it's like that."

"Wait," said Corky. "I've got ideas about a Discoverer's Club. But first I need help. Sam got loose again. When my dad finds out, he'll make me give him away."

"Hide him here!" said Pauline before he had a chance to say it himself. "He can be our mascot."

"I don't know how to bring him over. His cage is heavy."

"How about wheeling it down the road on Pauline's

skateboard?" This was Nogs's answer and, Corky thought, a great one.

"If we hurry, we can get him out before Mom is back from the station."

Pauline never went anyplace without her skateboard. Now she got it from the weeds, and they set off to rescue Sam.

It did not take long for four strong sixth-graders to hoist the cage onto the skateboard. Nogs turned out to be one of the best musclemen, in spite of his small size. Quickly, they shoved the cage down the alley, through the church parking lot, and toward the river.

"We'll never get across the highway in this traffic!" said Jim.

Boldly, Nogs stepped into the road the minute he saw a break in the stream of cars. "Now! Hold tight and move fast!"

The old lady driving the approaching car saw their plight. She stopped. Cars lined up behind her. Drivers began to honk. One man leaned out of his window and bellowed, "Get with it!" But she did not move until the parade was safe on the other side of the road.

"I'll put a lock on the door of our shack tomorrow," promised Jim. "Suppose someone does get curious and come in."

"I hate to leave a valuable snake alone out here," said Corky. "But this will have to do for a while until I think of something better."

"Why do you s'pose nobody uses this place?" Jim whispered.

Pauline shivered. "Let's not talk about it. The roof was

so full of holes before you fixed it that it probably didn't keep the rain out."

Corky felt queer inside. He changed the subject. "Nogs, do you have to walk home every time you miss the school bus?"

"Sure. It's fun. I've gotten to know people along the way. One grocer gives me an orange when he sees me." Nogs saw that his friends couldn't believe such a long walk was fun. He went on: "Bill gets home late most of the time. And there's nothing much except beans for supper. Why would I want to go home?"

"There're times I don't like to either," said Corky. He wasn't too sure he'd like to eat beans every night, though.

How hard it was going to be to face Dad tonight, and Mr. Mac tomorrow! He had already made up his mind to tell the principal who had rung the fire gong.

On the way home Corky rehearsed the way he would do it. And he tried out some different stories for Dad too.

When he reached the back porch of his house, he paused and braced himself for what was coming. But inside the kitchen, Dad was laughing fit to kill! How come?

Corky went in, perplexed. Between guffaws of laughter, his father gasped, "If that wasn't a clever way to shorten Millie's visit! Mabel, I couldn't have done better myself!"

When he saw Corky, he tried to look serious. "Hrrrumph! I understand your snake got loose again."

"Yes, sir."

"You recall what I told you the last time?"

"Yes, sir. Dad—I—he's already settled in a new home."

Mom looked startled. Dad's eyebrows raised in two question marks. "Where?"

"Some friends wanted him," stuttered Corky. "For their science club."

"How perfectly lovely!" said his mother, with a sigh of relief. "I'm sorry, dear. But you do know how we feel."

Before he washed for dinner, Corky went in and eyed the line of jars and tanks on his shelf. Frogs, garter snakes, Toby the lizard, Hasty the red racer . . . he would give every one of them away if Sam could come home!

That night Corky had a strange dream. Instead of being four feet long, Sam was a giant corn snake—at least eight or ten feet long. And he could talk back!

In the dream, Sam and Corky lived alone in the club shack. It was stocked with food for both of them. Peanut butter for Corky. Mice for Sam.

"The older grades are getting ready for the Grow Program," Corky told his dream pet. "Mr. Fairly, the Shop instructor, is filling the shed with lumber and nails and cans of varnish. You should see the new tools in the shop, Sam. Electric sanders. Drills."

"Didn't you hear the news?" asked Sam the dream snake. "You're in the Program!"

"No, Sam, not me. By the time things get rolling, I'll be out of that school."

He woke up and lay in the dark bedroom. What school would he go to if he got expelled? When you were expelled you didn't get to stay home and sit around the house. You had to go *somewhere*.

It was early yet. Mom and Dad were in the kitchen, talking. China clinked. Mom was making Dad his nightly cup of cocoa. The voices grew louder and louder.

"There's nothing the matter with that boy, Mabel."

Dad's voice was clear, like a deep bell. "City life doesn't agree with him—that's all. He can't get out and run the way he used to on the desert."

"He has a bike, Paul." Mom's voice was low for a woman. Often it got a little husky.

"At least we live on the edge of the city," she went on. "He can ride like the wind on the back streets when he wants to."

"It isn't the same thing, I tell you." The voices were softer now, arguing back and forth. Corky could not make out what they were saying.

Dad sounded homesick for eastern Oregon—great flat stretches of land under the blue bowl of sky, the river cutting through, the sun and the wind and the tumbleweeds.

Mom hadn't liked it. She had grown up in San Francisco and was used to the bustle of cities.

The next thing Dad said came out loud and clear. It was so unexpected that Corky sat bolt upright in bed, his fingers clenched into fists.

"Come hunting season, I'll take the boy out with me. He can use my old rifle. If I get an extra day off, we can go back to the eastern part of the state. Make him feel like a man to bag his own deer."

To watch one of those fleet brown creatures drop at the crack of a rifle? Corky's heart filled with grief. How could Dad, a gentle man under his burly crust, look forward to hunting season so? And Mom—the way she beamed with pride at the game he brought home!

How could they thrill over an animal shot down for sport and then get upset over Sam dining on a nice fat mouse? The Downs family didn't need venison to survive, the way Sam had to have his mouse.

"I won't go hunting with him!" said Corky to himself.

By the time he reached the River School the next morning, he had decided to see Mr. Mac the very first thing and get it over with.

It was early, but Mr. Mac was in his office. He glanced up from his papers with a look of pleasure that made Corky feel worse than ever.

The principal shoved his work to one side. He motioned to a chair. "More chess?" he teased.

"Not right n-now," stammered Corky. "Mr. Mac, I—I— I was the one who rang that false alarm yesterday. You see, I thought I might get into Grow if I acted so awful that Miss Puckett wouldn't want me in her room."

Mr. Mac tried to keep back a grin. His deep-set eyes twinkled.

"I looked out the window," said Corky. "I got the idea it would be fun to ring the primary bell ten minutes early so the kids would think—ah—think their recess was over. But I guess I got the wrong bell. I must have pushed the fire-alarm button instead."

The principal leaned back in his chair—so far back Corky thought he might go all the way over—and let out a whoop of laughter.

"Oh, my, boy! Oh, my!"

Corky's blank look set him chuckling again.

"You *thought* you set off a false alarm," Mr. Mac explained at last, as he blew his nose. "You see, at the beginning of the term, I like to have a fire drill and then surprise everyone with another a few days later to catch them off guard. I want both students and teachers to be able to respond quickly in an emergency. This way, I can check out what they have learned."

"You mean you rang the fire bell at the exact same time I rang the recess bell? I didn't set off a false alarm?" Corky gulped. All that worry for nothing!

Mr. Mac smiled. "Your joke backfired! Corky, you needn't worry about getting into the Grow Program. Your teacher and I have had you on the list from the beginning."

"Honest to Pete! Thanks, Mr. Mac! And about those tricks I tried . . ."

"Forget them," said the principal. "I've pulled a few in my day. But don't forget one other thing, Corky."

"Yes?"

"The game of chess I'm challenging you to. I'll see you at lunch hour someday soon."

CHAPTER 4

THE PECULIAR PRIZE

Of course Sam couldn't stay in the shack forever. Over the weekend, Corky did a lot of thinking about the problem. Maybe he could lend Sam to the zoo.

But when he called the zoo, the man who answered the phone said they did not take pets on loan. They did, however, accept various live animal gifts.

"No," said Corky. "That won't do." He hung up without bothering to explain.

Now he was worse off than ever before. No brother or sister to talk to—and no Sam. His other, smaller creatures did not seem to pay attention to what he said, the way Sam did, so he ended up talking out loud to himself.

"Corky Downs," he said in a severe voice, "you aren't such a dumb kid. Now settle down and think of *something!*"

On Monday the Grow Program started. Corky's name was on the list. Nogs was on it, and Skip Lacey too. Corky was so excited that, for a short time, he forgot to worry about Sam.

Grow Program girls were to meet Miss White in the Home Ec room at one. The Grow boys would be getting together with Mr. Fairly, the tall, broad-shouldered Shop instructor, at the same hour.

Would the morning ever go by? Corky was pleasantly surprised. Miss Lucy Puckett decided to hold her science class out of doors.

"Why not?" she asked. "It's a lovely day. We shall have a contest. Let's see who can find the greatest number of live creatures two inches long or under. You may explore the meadow behind the school. We'll call the swamp the boundary line."

Voices buzzed. Everyone wanted to be off at once.

"Wait!" said Miss Puckett. She unlocked the door of her supply cupboard and pulled out three cartons full of empty coffee cans and tomato-juice cans. Some of the boys helped her pass them around.

"The winner of the contest," said Miss Puckett, "may take my own baby iguana home for a week."

The buzz turned into an uproar. No one had known until this minute that little Miss Puckett had a real live iguana for a pet.

"Golly!" said Corky. An idea flew into his head. He would win the contest and take Miss Puckett's pet home. Iguanas were different from snakes. Not a bit wiggly, no, sirree! All they did was stretch out on a log or a stone and stare at you.

How big was a baby iguana? The full-grown one he had seen in a reptile museum was six feet long!

Several sixth-graders raced to the swamp and quickly filled their cans with small frogs.

"Look!" Nogs held out his hands. "I found this daddy longlegs, but if I put him in with my frog, won't the frog—"

"Yes," called Corky over his shoulder. "He will."

He found an earthworm he was sure would measure less than two inches. He found a beetle, a ladybug, a grasshopper, a spider, and two kinds of ants. Next he found a woolly-bear caterpillar and a garter snake. The snake was definitely not under the limit, but Corky wanted to keep it anyway. After that he found a green tree frog with suckers on its tiny feet. And a plain old water frog.

He nestled both of these in his shirt pocket where the garter snake could not reach them. Then, with the snake in one hand and his can in the other, he went back across the meadow to the school steps. Miss Puckett had started to examine and count specimens.

A teacher who had her own private iguana certainly would not get hysterical over a snake, so Corky showed his garter snake first.

"What a beauty, Benjamin! The snake does not count, of course, but every other specimen you found does. You've won the right to take Pokey, my iguana, home for a visit. And you get 100 percent in today's science lesson."

"Thanks, Miss Puckett!" Corky's blue eyes shone. "Can you bring him tomorrow?"

"His cage is on the backseat of my car, so you may take him today. That is, unless you need to get your parents' permission."

"Oh, no!" said Corky. "I've got all kinds of pets at home."

"Cheater!" jeered Skip with an angry glint in his eye.

"Some of your things didn't count," explained Corky. "Your five frogs were all alike. Take my ants. They're both

ants, but one guy's black and the other is a tiny red one."

Skip continued to scowl. Corky turned to listen to the teacher.

"I've had Pokey for such a short time," she was saying. "I don't want to let him visit our classroom yet. Later in the term, maybe. I am happy to lend him out for a week, because I would like him to get used to being handled by other people."

Pauline wrote Corky a note. "I'll get my skateboard so you can wheel his cage home."

A picture of Sam's large cage balanced on the skateboard popped into Corky's head. Suddenly he felt disloyal to Sam. He sent a thought-wave message out to the gray clubhouse near the river: "Never mind, Sam, old boy. Just remember, I'm doing this for you!"

Promptly at one, he went to the Grow meeting. Skip Lacey arrived with a scowl still pulling his eyebrows together.

"Who wants to be in Grow?" he said. "Mr. Mac is putting us to work so he can save some money."

But most of the other boys, like Corky, were looking forward to the afternoon.

Mr. Fairly, Grow director, was a quite different man from Mr. Fairly, Shop instructor. In Shop, he talked nothing but woodworking projects. Out by the shed, with his shirt sleeves rolled up and the sun shining on his brawny arms, he talked about lots of things.

He told the boys about his life before he was a teacher. Mostly he had grown up on houseboats. He and his wife and his daughters lived on a houseboat now.

Corky and Nogs looked at each other.

The first Grow project was digging holes for fence posts.

Mr. Fairly did not stand around overseeing the boys. He grabbed a spade and dug three postholes himself. While he made the dirt fly, he taught them some sea chanteys he had learned in the Merchant Marines. Before they were through that afternoon, they knew the words to "Yeo, Heave Ho!" and "Blow the Man Down."

Mr. Fairly's forehead glistened with sweat. Corky had two blisters. Perspiration streamed down his grimy neck. It made his shirt stick to his body.

Nogs had blisters too. When they sat on the grass to rest, he sucked them to cool them down. "I wish I lived on a houseboat," he told Corky between sucks. "Jim's family has had theirs for four years."

"Jim lives on a houseboat?" Corky was astonished. "Why does he keep it such a secret?"

Skip hooted. "He's ashamed, stupid! Houseboats are the cheapest way to live."

Corky was embarrassed. Mr. Fairly was working on a posthole next to the one Skip was struggling with. The Shop instructor hummed softly. He strode off and came back with a measuring stick.

"Splendid work, Corky, Nogs, Roy, Fred, Mike. But, Skip, your two holes are only a foot and a half deep. They need to measure twice that. Get busy!"

He turned to Nogs with a smile. "You're right. Houseboats are great places to live. Cozy. Handy if you like water-skiing and messing around in boats."

Corky wiped his face on his shirt sleeve. He was so thirsty he couldn't stand it any longer. He went inside to get a drink at the fountain in the front hall. No one was around, so he let the cool water spurt into his face and hair. He emerged dripping from the building and stood on the steps. From here you could look across the river at Mount St. Helens. The distant peak looked like a mound of vanilla ice cream.

"Well, Corky," rumbled a voice. "How do you like our new program?"

Startled, he turned to face Mr. Mac. No way to hide his wet hair, which was plastered to his forehead in sticky red spikes. "I like it fine," he said. "Mr. Mac, I get to take Miss Puckett's iguana home for a week!"

Mr. Mac look amused. "That Lucy Puckett! What will your parents say?"

"They won't care," said Corky. But now that the time was getting near, he was beginning to wonder! "I collect reptiles."

"Interesting that you should find yourself in Miss Puckett's class. You two should get along famously!"

What did the principal mean? No time to ask. The bell was ringing. Now he could go see Pokey!

Many sixth-graders stayed after school to see the teacher's strange pet. Pokey was a pale-green, warty creature. He had a few faint blackish markings. He had spines on his back and chin.

"He looks like an old man in a wrinkled suit that's way too big!" laughed Corky. He was relieved to see that the iguana was small.

Pokey was lying on a branch in his glass tank. He grasped it firmly with his long, long toes. His front legs were much shorter than his hind ones.

But his tail was longer than he was.

"Pokey is only an eight-inch baby," said Miss Puckett. "When he grows up, that tail will measure nearly four feet, compared to a two-foot head and trunk. I plan to donate him to the zoo before that happens."

She looked worried when she saw Pauline's skateboard. "Corky, this tank is so expensive that I'd prefer to drop you off in my car."

"Could we go up the back alley?" asked Corky. "My bedroom is at the back of the house, near the kitchen."

Mom would have to get acquainted with Pokey slowly.

All the way home, Corky hoped the family Chevy would not be in the driveway. "Please, Mom," he begged silently, "don't be home!"

Good! The car was gone!

Politely, he let the teacher help him carry the cage inside. They parked it on the worktable in the empty spot usually occupied by Sam's large box.

Corky found himself explaining what was in every jar and cage on his shelf. Miss Puckett seemed really interested. He told her about the rattler he had killed on a camping trip with Dad. He showed her his red racer and told her about Sam.

"He's off on a visit, just like your Pokey," Corky said. "In fact, I'd better go see how he's doing right now."

It was the only way he could think of to get her out of the house before Mom walked in.

"Pokey's neat!" he said at the door. "I won't forget to give him water and bits of orange. Really, Miss Puckett, I'll take good care of him."

Pokey looked comfortable resting on his branch. Not a

muscle twitched. His eyes stared quietly at his new sur-
roundings. He was so ugly that Corky felt a twinge of un-
easiness. But Mom didn't fuss over toads or lizards, so she
probably wouldn't have any trouble getting used to an
iguana.

Corky closed the door to his bedroom so that Mom would
not see Pokey before he had a chance to explain about win-
ning the contest.

At the shack, the club members were waiting for him.

"You lucky bum!" said Pauline. "How come your mom'll
let you keep Pokey when she doesn't like Sam? He looks
fierce!"

"Mom hasn't seen him yet," Corky told her. "But he's a
vegetarian, so I don't guess she'll mind. It was the mice
Sam ate that got on her nerves."

He unlocked his pet's cage and stroked him. Today Nogs
felt brave enough to hold the snake for a few minutes. Then
Jim, then Pauline.

"He feels *good!*" she shouted in surprise. "Kind of mus-
cly!"

"What was your idea about a Discoverer's Club?" asked
Jim.

Corky told his idea. "We could do *real* scientific research," he explained. "We could call ourselves the D.C.s."

"Sounds good!" said Jim. The others thought so too.

"Before we hunt for cocoons and other things, let's eat
some of the cupcakes Pauline made in Home Ec," said
Nogs. As usual, his mind was on food.

"They're burned on the bottom," she said with modesty.
She brought out the black-bottomed cupcakes and passed
them around.

Single file, they trailed out the door.

"Ouch! Next time I'll bring my jackknife to cut these brambles!" Carefully, Jim held a long prickly branch between thumb and forefinger to let the others pass by.

By ducking and crawling, they came to the far edge of the thick tangle. The vines there drooped heavily, loaded with plump, ripe blackberries.

For a little while, the discoverers forgot their scientific mission and stuffed themselves. At last Nogs rolled his purple tongue around the corners of his mouth. "Can't eat another one," he sighed.

Corky did not hear. He was at the top of a tree investigating a nest. "It's an old crow's nest!" he called. "Help me get it down, Jim!"

An hour later he jogged home in high spirits. What a day! One hundred in Science. The beginning of Grow. A secret shack as a hideaway for Sam. And an iguana to visit for the week.

He burst through the front door shouting, "I got one hundred in Science today!" Then he stopped short and stood trembling.

There was Mom lying pale-faced on the couch. Dad was kneeling by her side, holding an ice bag on her forehead.

"What's the . . . what happened?"

"Oh, Corky!" murmured his mother sorrowfully.

"Corky Downs!" said his father in a choked voice. "You go get that *baby dinosaur* out of this house! Your mother merely opened your door to stick your laundry on your bed and . . ."

"I fainted," Mom apologized. "I've never done such a thing before. I'm not the frail type. But, Corky—how could you?"

CHAPTER 5

AN ORDEAL FOR SAM

Back to the sixth-grade room went Pokey, escorted by Corky and Mr. Downs, at eight thirty in the morning.

"I'm warning you, son." Mr. Downs huffed and puffed as they carried the heavy cage up the school steps. "If this school gives you nothing but fence-post digging classes or ... or lessons in iguana baby-sitting, I'll ... I'll transfer you to another school. Yes, sirree, that's exactly what I'll do!"

But he looked carefully at the maps and pictures and articles on Miss Puckett's bulletin board. And through the window, Corky saw him walk over and look at the new fence. Then he got into his Nifty Service truck and drove off to work.

Transfer to a different school? Ugh! But Dad's bark was usually worse than his bite. Corky shrugged. He thought, instead, about the science unit on pet personalities that his class was starting.

Today Miss Puckett made a long list of the pets each pupil planned to bring to school for a day's visit.

An unusual pet like Sam would cause a lot of excitement. There were so many facts to tell about him! Maybe, Corky thought, he could get Miss Puckett to let Sam visit for two or three weeks instead of one little bitty day.

The next day, Pauline stopped by with her skateboard to help Corky wheel the cage from the shack to the school.

"Hurry up, Cork! I want to leave enough time to go back and get Snow White, my kitten."

"What happens if someone else brings a dog?" asked Corky.

"Miss Puckett has that list, silly. The only dog on it is Mike's big poodle, Tar. He's used to cats, so he won't chase her."

By the time they got the cage to the door of the class-room, Miss Puckett was already telling everyone where to put his pets. Corky could see that most of them were small caged creatures like hamsters, and parrakeets, and turtles, and white mice.

Something stirred deep inside of him when he saw Fred's white mice. "They would sure make some good meals for you, old boy," he whispered through the screened side of Sam's cage. "And to think I have to pay thirty-five cents a head!"

Jim Mahony helped him lift the cage over to the low wide shelf under the windows. Corky was ready for a few gasps, but not for the scene that followed when he unlocked the door to show Sam off.

One silly girl had a fit worse than Aunt Milly's! It was Carla Rumple, a big, gawky kid with a loud voice. "Help!" she shrieked. "Help! Help! Lemme outa here!"

Her arms paddled the air and knocked over Fred's mouse cage. The door popped open and out leaped half a dozen white mice. They scampered in every direction at once.

Carla took a flying leap onto a desk. *"Eeeeeeeeeee!"*

She sounded as if she were getting shots for nine different diseases at once!

Children fell to their knees and crawled up and down the aisles, trying to catch the mice. Mike's poodle barked. Roy's parrakeet twittered. Pauline arrived with her cat.

Above the racket, Miss Lucy Puckett's calm voice commanded, "Benjamin, quick! The classroom door!"

Corky ran to slam it. Someone else shouted, "Let Snow White down to do the job, Pauline! Or how about Sam?"

The boy was teasing, but Fred looked horrified. The hubbub died down to whispers. Everyone waited to see what the teacher would do.

"Carla, get down! You can see for yourself that Benjamin's snake cage has a padlock on it." Spots of color burned on the teacher's cheekbones. The way her dark eyes danced made Corky wonder if she might be thinking the escaped mice were a good joke.

"You wouldn't let your snake eat my mice, would you, Corky?" pleaded Fred. "I couldn't bear to think of Jasper or Silky Ears inside of a snake."

"Sam doesn't eat mice that have names," explained Corky. It sounded screwy, but he could not think of a better way to say what he meant. Whenever he had to keep a mouse in a cage until Sam was in an eating mood, he was careful not to name it. Once the beady-eyed, whiskery little thing had a name of its own—why, then it became a real pet instead of a dinner.

Corky was thinking that Sam had not had a good juicy mouse for ever so long. But out loud he said, "Your pets are safe, Fred, really."

The class calmed down now. Miss Puckett sent a messenger to the school kitchen. Soon he returned with a piece of cheese. This she broke into bits and placed at different points around the room. "Now we shall see what happens before the day is over," she said. "Pauline, you'd better leash Snow White with this strong nylon cord, just in case."

Corky checked his pocket. Ah, there was the key to Sam's padlock! It seemed to be bent on the end, so he took it out and looked at it.

Yes, the tip needed fixing before he could use it again. Carefully, he wiggled it around in the crack made by the hinges on his desk lid. Then he dropped it inside the desk.

He did not want to leave the key home in a trouser pocket when someday he might need it in a hurry at school.

Corky had the feeling he was being watched. Nervously

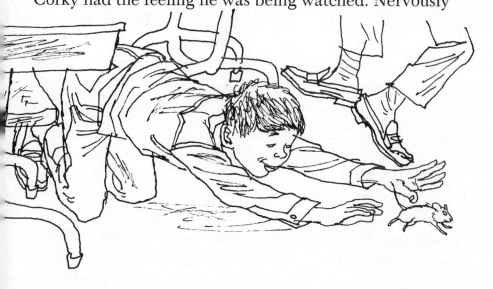

he looked up. All eyes were glued to Miss Puckett, who was announcing that the first report would be given by Jim Mahony. To be on the safe side, Corky hid the key under his arithmetic book and began to listen to Jim.

Jim's pet didn't come to class. It was a wild duck named Waddles. One spring Mr. Mahony had set the broken wing of a baby mallard. Since that time, the duck, Waddles, had been a pet of the Mahony household. He would plod right into the kitchen where Jim was eating breakfast and take food out of his hand! He especially liked shredded-wheat biscuits.

After Jim finished, Roy told about his parrakeet. Then Pauline gave a report on Snow White. The parrakeet report was boring, but Pauline's was better. You wouldn't think a kitten could do some of the tricks Snow White knew how to do. Like pawing goldfish out of a garden pond. But, was that a trick or a kitten's instinct? Right then and there, the report stopped and a class discussion began.

Corky heaved a happy sigh. Today was a special day, the only day pets would be allowed to visit the classroom— except, he hoped, for Sam. The whole day would be nothing but one long science class.

"And now Benjamin will report on snakes," announced Miss Puckett.

Corky took the key out of his desk and shuffled to the front of the room. His cheeks got red. What if he suddenly forgot everything he planned to tell about Sam?

"Many people are frightened of snakes," Miss Puckett was saying. "That is a fear caused by ignorance. The snake has an interesting history, and a snake can make a fine pet! Reptiles go back 250 million years to the Mesozoic period.

Perhaps Benjamin will want to begin his report by telling us the difference between a reptile and an amphibian."

That was easy.

"A reptile," began Corky, "is a cold-blooded land animal that has a backbone and gets around by crawling. An amphibian . . . I *think* an amphibian has a backbone and is cold-blooded but lives part of the time in the water and part of the time on land. Like a frog."

"Right!" said Miss Puckett.

"Could I take Sam out and hold him if I promise I won't let him go?" Now Corky's mind was full of facts about snakes.

The teacher nodded. And she was the first person to reach out a finger and stroke Sam's back!

"In spite of the way it looks, a snake's skin does not feel slimy or even scaly," she told the class.

"They're good pets because they need very little care," put in Corky. "They can go for ten days without food as long as you leave a dish of water in their cage."

He told the class how Sam could shed his skin so neatly that you could see the place where his eyeballs had been. He told them that a snake has four jaws hinged together in such an elastic way that it can devour a very large prey.

"A friend of mine in Africa once found the antlers of a deer inside of a snake's belly," Miss Puckett told them.

Corky looked at her, surprised.

He went on to tell about the big rattler he and Dad had killed. He promised to bring the rattles to school, if no one jumped on the desks or screamed. He glared at Carla.

You could hear a pin drop. Every student was listening. At the end, Corky said anyone who liked could come up and hold Sam for a few minutes. Skip Lacey stayed at his desk, but Nogs came, and Roy, and Jim Mahony. Pauline was the only girl who wanted to hold Sam. She reached out bravely and took him. She didn't even wince when he flicked his forked tongue.

"An excellent report," said Miss Puckett. "Benjamin, the *World of Reptiles and Amphibians* book is in our school library. It is so large that it would count for a whole month of book reports if you wish to use it."

"Gee, thanks, Miss Puckett!" Corky put Sam back in his cage. "Watch this." The children crowded around to see how Sam could find his way back into his upside-down flowerpot.

"He can't see too well, and he isn't too smart," admitted Corky. "So, watch what he does first. He always wants to try to squeeze through the little hole at the top of the pot instead of through the broken place at the side."

Finally Sam gave up trying to get through the wrong hole. Just as his tail disappeared from sight, Fred reported, "I've caught three mice!"

During the talks he had been watching. Whenever one of his very tame pets found a bit of cheese, it was easy for Fred to reach out and get him.

"They aren't afraid of my hand," boasted Fred. "Except for Silky Ears. He's still missing. He's more shy than the others."

When Corky came back from Grow Program that afternoon, every mouse was safely in the cage. The children were collecting their hamsters and parrakeets and other pets from the shelf. It was time to go home.

"Benjamin, a snake is an easy creature to keep in the

classroom for scientific observation," said Miss Puckett. "Could Sam visit here for several days?"

"Oh, yes, Miss Puckett, for weeks and *weeks!*" Corky told her happily. He hadn't even had to ask! Delighted, he hurried to the shelf to check his pet's water dish.

"For Pete's sake!" he hollered. "Oh, jumping jiminy! The padlock's gone! And Sam has escaped!"

"Oh, no!" shrieked the children that were left. Luckily, Carla Rumple had already gone home.

"Oh, yes!" insisted Corky. His classmates did not know, but *he* knew and Miss Puckett knew that snakes travel fast. By now Sam could be anyplace in the whole school! Neither of them said it out loud.

"We'll help you look," said Fred. Corky knew he must be glad that his mice were safely locked in their cage.

"No, no!" Miss Puckett had had quite enough pet troubles for one day. "Every one of you is to leave. Benjamin and I will find Sam."

"We'll meet you-know-where," whispered Nogs. "Hope you find him!"

"We'll find him O.K.," said Corky between his teeth. "See you later."

Up and down the aisles they went, sometimes walking slowly, sometimes crawling on hands and knees. Miss Puckett went over and climbed up on the wide shelf.

"Snakes climb, Corky. Ahhh-Choo! These moldings are dusty. I guess Noah is too little and old to reach them easily."

As if he'd heard his name, the bent old janitor appeared at the classroom door. "Sumpin' wrong, Miss Puckett? Can I help?"

Usually Corky liked to watch Noah. His skin was leathery. One eye squinted shut when he talked. He was a funny man. But today Corky couldn't smile.

"My pet snake got loose," muttered Corky.

Noah joined the search.

"Go look in the coatroom again," urged Miss Puckett.

"There's nothing in there except a sweater of Carla's and Roy's Little League baseball cap," Corky told her. Just the same he went back into the coatroom and looked again.

Carla Rumple's heavy blue sweater with saggy pockets hung limp on a coat hook. Corky scowled at it and shook his fist. "Snake hater!" he said.

"Do you suppose Sam escaped because you forgot to lock his cage, or because somebody wanted to play a prank and let him out?" asked Miss Puckett.

"I *know* that cage was locked!" said Corky. "I—I took the key out of my pocket this morning and wiggled it around in the crack in my desk. It was bent. When it was fixed, why, I stuck it in the corner of my desk. It isn't there now, and it isn't in my pockets. Besides, Miss Puckett, the padlock is gone from the cage. Snakes can escape all right, but they can't walk off with padlocks."

"Then it must have happened while you were at Grow."

The teacher was right. That meant it couldn't have been Skip Lacey. He'd been at Grow with Corky all afternoon.

"Benjamin, I must go home," said Miss Puckett at last. "Your snake has been loose such a very short time, he could hardly have found his way out of this room. Come along now. Take one of those permission slips for our Thursday trip to the zoo—on my desk there. I'll lock the classroom door. Who knows? Perhaps your pet will be waiting for us in plain sight in the morning!"

She sounded cheerful, as if she really thought it might happen.

Corky Downs didn't feel cheerful. "Oh, gee whillikers!" he mumbled. Then, remembering his manners, "But thanks anyway for all the looking you and Noah did."

He grabbed a permission slip and crumpled it into his back pocket. Who wanted to go to the zoo now, when Sam was lost? Outside the school building, he kicked a dirt clod and wiped his hand across his eyes.

He didn't feel like going over to the clubhouse. Jim had been elected class treasurer and the D.C.s were going to plan a way to sell more candy bars than any of the other sixth-graders. The money from the candy bars was for field trips—lots of small trips like the one to the zoo. But mostly it was for a special big trip at the end of the school year, a week-long class trip to eastern Oregon.

Corky had never been in a school that took trips like that. It sounded great. He often dreamed about the way he would show everyone else how to hunt for snakes when they camped on the desert.

The only thing on his mind now, though, was Sam. Who could have been mean enough to let Sam loose?

CHAPTER 6

SURPRISE! SURPRISE!

Dinner stuck in his throat. He couldn't sleep. When he shook his head at breakfast, Mom frowned and felt his forehead.

"Corky, are you sick?"

"Just not hungry, Mom." To please her, he choked down a piece of buttered toast and a glass of milk. It would be terrible if Mom decided he wasn't well enough to go to school today. He had to go to school. He had to find Sam!

"Pauline says she doesn't want to be a D.C.," reported Jim as soon as he saw Corky hit the playground. "She was acting cross and queer."

Corky brushed him aside. He didn't want to hear about candy bar sales or Pauline or anything else. As soon as the bell rang he rushed into the sixth-grade classroom and over to the snake cage. If only Miss Puckett had found Sam and put him back! No such luck!

Everyone was sorry about Sam. Everyone, that is, except Carla. She stuck out her tongue when Miss Puckett wasn't looking.

"You shoulda known better than to bring that dangerous snake to school!" she said under her breath when she went by Corky's desk. "Makes me sick to my stomach."

"Oh, shut up!" said Corky.

"Children, children! Do stop whispering and open your math books to page sixty-seven!" Miss Puckett was trying to carry on as if nothing had happened. It was hard to do. She knew, and her pupils knew, that somewhere a four-foot orange-and-brown snake was lurking!

"That snake *could* have gotten out of the room and down the hall," the teacher told the class after the math lesson. "But I doubt it. Surely we would have seen that long creature glide across the floor right under our very noses."

"Not if half of us were in Grow and the rest were looking at the blackboard," Corky said glumly.

"I believe he is in this room," said Miss Puckett firmly. "I've never seen the day when every single pupil was looking at the blackboard so hard that a snake could escape without being seen."

She tried to bring everyone's attention to spelling lesson number thirteen.

"Did you remember to look under his flowerpot?" wrote Nogs in a note.

"Of course I did," Corky scribbled angrily on a sheet of paper.

"Hope he's gone for good," mumbled Skip in the seat beside Corky. "Snakes make me feel creepy."

Corky wanted to yell, "There he is, right now, under your desk!" just to see Skip jump. But he felt so bad about Sam that he couldn't even tease.

Jim wrote a note and so did Fred and Mike and Roy.

Pauline was not in school.

"She sure acted huffy when we were planning out who would take what block for the candy sale yesterday," whispered Jim as he and Corky wrote spelling words on the board. "She didn't stay at the shack for more'n five minutes."

Corky was so upset about Sam that he couldn't even spell a simple word like "circle."

It came time for the unit on animal personalities. Miss Puckett asked the class to list things they had noticed about the pets who had visited school.

"For instance," she said, "could Fred's mice do anything that an ordinary house mouse or field mouse couldn't do? Had they *learned* anything by being pets?"

"Yes!" said one boy. "They had learned not to be afraid when a human hand picked them up."

"Right," said Miss Puckett. "What about Benjamin's snake?"

"He wasn't so smart!" jeered Skip. "*Any* snake, even a little bitty garter snake, might crawl through a broken place in a flowerpot!"

"Are snakes dumber than mice?" asked someone else.

Corky's cheeks reddened to match his hair. "Maybe they aren't smart, the way a kitten or dog is," he said. "But snakes are pretty, and they have *instinct*. Look at the way Sam knows how to shed his skin! And why does he eat a mouse, but then he won't touch a—well—something like a frog?"

Skip could make you so sore! So what if he could prove he was in the Grow Program all afternoon? He was nasty enough to bribe somebody else to snitch the key and let Sam loose.

Corky pretended he was a snake. Where would he hide? Somewhere warm and cozy. Down behind the books in the bookcase at the back of the room? In the trash at the bottom of the big metal wastepaper basket? Oh, horrors! What if Noah had thrown Sam out when he emptied the basket last night? What did he do with all the trash, anyway?

"Benjamin, do pay attention now!" Miss Puckett broke into his thoughts for the umpteenth time. "Thinking about that snake all day won't find him for you. You know he's probably curled up in a warm corner having a snooze."

She didn't have to get so biggety! Just because she had an iguana and had read some books about reptiles didn't mean she knew everything.

"It is time to get ready for lunch," said Miss Puckett. "Please put books and papers inside your desks."

"I'm gonna go home for lunch today," said Carla Rumple in a low voice. "I don't want to stick around school with that—that *monster* loose!"

"Pooh!" said Corky. "Maybe he's hiding because he's scared of a face like yours."

Would he ever find Sam again?

The day was cool and breezy. Sixth-graders hurried into the coatroom to grab sweaters and jackets so they could go right out to play ball after lunch. Carla came out of the coatroom in her droopy blue sweater, still muttering. "I hope your old snake climbed into one of the ceiling lights and got fried!"

"Yah!" Corky jostled hard against her. "How would he get across the ceiling? Tell me that!"

Some of the kids had left. Some were standing around

to see if Corky Downs would really fight a girl.

"Oh, *yoweeeeeee!* Aye-yi-oweeeeeeeeeeeeeee! Help! Murder!" Suddenly, Carla began to dance up and down and wave her arms around. Today there was no mouse cage to knock over, but she did jostle Nogs so that he lost his balance.

Nogs fell to his knees as he grabbed what dropped out of Carla's wildly waving hands.

"It's Sam!" he shouted. "Look, Corky, Sam must have been asleep in the pocket of Carla's sweater!"

"It's Sam! It's Sam!" Corky sang out. "Oh, Sam, how *are* you?"

It was plain to see that Sam had not been hurt. He was sluggish and sleepy, a bit cross from having his nap disturbed.

"We should have thought to look in Carla's sweater!" Miss Puckett had come to the door of the coatroom to see what all the racket was about. "It's not the first time I've known a snake to take a snooze in somebody's pocket!"

All the other children had gone to lunch, but Corky and the teacher stood admiring the snake, who was now hanging quietly around his owner's neck.

"He needs about two mice, Miss Puckett," said Corky. "He hasn't had any for ages. And could I have permission to run down to the hardware store and buy a new padlock for his cage? Even encyclopedias on the lid might not be safe."

"I happen to have a small padlock in my desk," Miss Puckett told him. "I think some of your friends would probably like to see how a corn snake stalks his prey, so you may bring a mouse tomorrow." She smiled and added,

"Sam may have his dinner during recess so that your class-mates can leave if they want to."

Corky knew she was thinking of Carla. One thing still bothered him. Who had been mean enough to unlock Sam's cage? He was going to find out.

The D.C.s met at the shack after school. "I bet Skip Lacey bribed somebody to do it while he was in Grow," said Corky.

"But who?" asked Nogs.

"You're not being fair," said Jim. "Maybe Skip didn't have anything to do with it. Anyway, Sam is found and he's fine, so let's forget it. We've got this candy sale to worry about. Now that Pauline doesn't want to be a D.C., we'll have to work harder."

"I bet Pauline'll change her mind," said Nogs. "She wasn't feeling good yesterday, that's all."

Corky's mind was still on Sam. "Sam is *not* fine," he told the others. "He looked O.K. when we first found him, but he wouldn't even crawl into his flowerpot when I put him back in his cage. He's very sluggish. Something's wrong."

"He might have forgotten how," said Jim. "You said yourself that snakes aren't the brightest."

The next day Sam refused a good mouse dinner at recess. Corky grew more worried. "He's not ready to shed again. It can't be that, Miss Puckett."

"A month is not too long a time for a snake to go without eating dinner," said Miss Puckett thoughtfully. "Except for the fact that Sam was used to eating once a week. Benjamin, you have my permission to take your pet to the zoo when we go tomorrow. Maybe the curator of the Reptile House can tell us if anything is wrong."

Just in case Sam had needed some time to recover, Corky offered him a mouse the next morning before the bus took off for the field trip to the zoo. But Sam turned away.

"All this fuss about a silly snake!" said Pauline. She had been absent from school only one day, but she had been acting huffy ever since.

Could she be wheedled into staying in the Discoverer's Club?

"Heck, no. It's too boring. I'd rather go skateboarding." That was all Corky could get out of her. She hurried out to the bus. Corky tied Sam into his collecting bag.

Pauline had saved him a seat next to Jim at the very back of the bus! All the way to the zoo she amused the whole bus with her tales of skateboarding tricks.

"You know how flat it is down by the river?" she asked. "Well, at the garage in town where my dad works, it's better. The hill there goes shwoop-dee-doop!"

Pauline's hand shwoop-dee-dooped. The bus took a curve. She lost her balance, toppled sideways, and there she was, sitting on Corky's lap!

Her cheeks got pink. She bubbled over with giggles. Not Corky Downs! He was crimson, but he certainly was not laughing!

"Watch out, will ya?" he yelped. "You're squashing Sam!" He gave her a powerful shove and almost boosted her into Jim's lap. She caught herself in time.

"Corky's girl friend! Ha, ha, ha! Going steady?"

Every kid in the bus took up the yell.

Redder than ever, Corky turned to Jim. "How's your houseboat?" he mumbled. It sounded silly.

But Jim surprised him by saying, "Mom told me I could

invite three fellows to spend the night in a couple of weeks. Can you come, Corky?"

"We're here! Pile out, everyone!" shouted a boy up front.

Corky would have to hear about the houseboat party later. He pretended not to see Pauline trying to catch up with him and apologize. He went through the turnstile into the zoo grounds.

Miss Puckett paused with Miss White, the pretty Home Ec teacher who had come along to help. "Which way?"

"The Reptile House!" shouted Corky above the noise.

Miss White's face paled, but Lucy Puckett never blinked. "Those who wish to come with Benjamin and me may do so. The rest of you may go with Miss White."

Pauline was coming along to the Reptile House with Jim and Nogs and several other boys.

Miss Puckett led them to a door at the back of the building. She knocked. A tall young man came to the door. His glasses gave him an owlish look.

"We would like the curator to look at a pet corn snake whose owner thinks he is sick," Miss Puckett explained. "No appetite. Sluggish. Oh, by the way, I am Lucy Puckett, sixth-grade teacher at the River School."

An exciting, unexpected, wonderful thing happened. The owlish young man cried, "Don't tell me! You couldn't be, but, yes, you are indeed—Lucy Puckett, daughter of the famous Dr. Emmett C. Puckett, explorer, herpetologist, naturalist! I'd know you anywhere, after watching the TV account of the way you helped your father in his African studies!"

The children stared, openmouthed. Miss Puckett blushed.

"My father *is* a famous herpetologist," she admitted. "I have not mentioned it at school because I want my pupils to learn to do their own research rather than sit back and listen to my adventures."

The young man said his name was Bob Elton. He was an assistant in the Reptile House. "The curator is away today," he told Corky. "But perhaps I can help."

"What's herpe-herpetology?" asked Jim.

"It is the study of reptiles," said Miss Puckett.

Bob Elton set the snake under a lamp on a table. He examined him carefully. He asked about the size of Sam's cage, how much screen wire it had, and other details.

"He certainly is a magnificent creature!" he said at last. "I don't see anything wrong with your pet's throat. His skin looks healthy too. I've known snakes to refuse a meal for as long as two or three months. In cool weather like this, do you keep a light bulb shining into the cage?"

"No," said Corky slowly. "I thought the room was warm enough."

"Try rigging up a strong light bulb close to the top screen. You can buy a thermometer in the dime store and hang it inside. When it registers above 85 or 90 degrees, that is good."

"Thank you!" Corky stuffed Sam into his bag, delighted to know he was not ill. "Miss Puckett, did you know Sam's cage was too cool?"

"I thought it might be, Benjamin. You see, Portland weather is quite a bit colder than eastern Oregon's. And, anyway, something else might have been wrong too. I'm glad you brought Sam in for a checkup."

Bob Elton locked the back room. He gave the children a

special tour of the Reptile House. Corky's brain was full of questions. Do anacondas ever grow thirty feet long as some books claim? What about the deadly venom that squirts through a cobra's hollow fangs—is it any different from other snake venom? And could Bob Elton tell him how you get to be a herpetologist?

Miss Puckett and Bob talked and talked, telling adventures and discussing places they'd been on field trips. Corky could not get a word in. He wandered around with Pauline and the boys, looking through the glass fronts of the cages. There were pythons and boas, and rattlers and coral snakes.

It would have been fun to spend the whole afternoon there. But suddenly Miss Puckett said, "My stars! Miss White will be wondering what has happened to us! Thank you, Mr. Elton, we must be on our way."

"Come back," he called after them. "And, Benjamin, please let me know what effect a light has on your snake."

Miss White and the rest of the class were watching a zoo man feed the giraffes. The man leaned out of a high window and tossed carrots, heads of lettuce, and whole onions into the pen. Crunch went an onion!

"Mercy!" gasped Miss White. "Think of that!"

But Corky's mind was on reptiles, not on onion-eating giraffes.

"I'm going to be a herpe-whatever-you-call-it, too," said Pauline on the way home. "If Miss Puckett can go to Africa to hunt snakes, I guess I can!"

Corky shot her a disgusted look. Girls!

"Not me," said Jim. "I'm going to be a Merchant Marine

and go around the world. Corky, don't forget to ask your mother about my houseboat party."

"My teacher is famous. Well, her father is, anyhow," Corky told his mother when he got home. He sat on the kitchen stool, his heels hooked over the bottom rung, and watched her roll out a batch of biscuits. He told her about the onion-eating giraffe and the camel that spit when people got too close. He did not mention snakes.

"Sounds wonderful, dear." Mom gave him a floury pat. "Now run in and wash for dinner. Perhaps you'll be a famous scientist someday yourself."

"Herpetologist," he corrected her under his breath. When he was out of earshot, he said it again: "Dr. Benjamin Downs, herpetologist." It sounded great!

CHAPTER 7

AN EXCITING NIGHT

"I hope you don't mind Skip coming." Jim spoke in a low voice so the Lacey boy would not hear. "His mother met my mother in the grocery store and asked if he could spend the night. His mother and dad have to go to Seattle."

"That's O.K., Jim," said Nogs.

"Yeah, I guess," muttered Corky. He wasn't sure. "Don't you tell him I'm bringing Sam along in the collecting bag."

He had asked permission to bring Sam to the houseboat party. He had not had much chance to hold his snake or visit with him lately. And it made him uneasy to leave Sam in his cage at school over the weekends. He did not want anything else to happen to his pet.

Skip came up lugging his sleeping bag. Jim was going to lend an extra one to Nogs. Corky had his own bag, as well as a flashlight, an army canteen, a ghost-story book, and a few other things Jim had said to bring.

"A big wind storm is on the way," Mrs. Mahony told them when she came to pick them up. Corky felt that he would be right at home with this large, motherly woman. She was dressed in her husband's navy pea jacket, a pair of warm slacks, and some fur-lined boots.

"Made a batch of brownies and a pan of cinnamon buns," she went on. "There's potato chips and pop for after dinner. But I'll warm you with a pot of cocoa when you get home. Say, there's one tree down already! Wind's blowing up a fit!"

In the front seat of the car, Jim hugged his baby sister Jancie. "We'll have fun! We can play we're marooned on a desert island!"

Rain poured down in sheets. The sky shone a queer gunmetal gray. The river looked like a bar of polished steel. Some trees were bare, but here and there a few spots of color dotted the lowlands.

Mrs. Mahony parked the car in the lot at the top of the moorage. The boys stepped into the November dusk, bracing themselves against wind and rain.

"Watch that ramp! It's slick!" warned Jim.

Skip held tightly to the rail, but Corky and Nogs skidded after Jim until Nogs fell down. The hood of Nogs's parka had blown off and his head was drenched. He'd visited Jim before. "Jim's is the red one at the very end of the floating walk," he said.

"Did you see that houseboat with the freezer on the deck?" asked Corky. "And the one next to it had a motorcycle parked on it!"

"We're here," said Jim. "Take a giant step."

Corky's long legs jumped first, then Nogs's shorter ones. Skip paused, not willing to admit he was scared. Then he too landed on the slippery deck of the houseboat.

They crowded through the door and stood dripping on a scatter rug. The largest room of the houseboat was the living room. It had green carpeting on the floor and starched white curtains at the windows. Corky's sharp eyes saw a hi-fi like his father's and a bookshelf loaded with books.

He had kept Sam's bag under his windbreaker. It was still nice and dry. When no one was looking, he handed the bag to Jim and Jim whisked it into his bedroom. He did not seem to want to let his mother know that one of the guests was a four-foot snake!

"Hang your wet jackets on the rack over the tub," called Mrs. Mahony. She was a quick worker. She had already unwrapped baby Jancie from the quilt and stuck her into her crib. Now she was out in the small galley kitchen warming the cocoa. When Corky went over and stood in the doorway to watch, she smiled.

"You can reach whatever you need without moving!" he said.

"Did you notice the bedrooms, Corky? Real beds and everything!" For once in his life, Skip hadn't made one single wisecrack.

Jim's bedroom was the best place on the boat. He had covered the wall with maps. Africa, China, Europe, Iceland, and many more. In the middle was a big map of the world.

"I'm going to join the Merchant Marines and go to all these places," Jim reminded them.

Corky stared hard at the continent of Africa. It seemed so far away! But, then, if Miss Puckett had been to Africa, why couldn't he get there too?

A fishnet was hanging on the other wall. Caught in it were treasures Jim had collected. Starfish from the ocean beach, a round green glass buoy from a Japanese net, old bottles, shells, bits of driftwood.

From a hook, Jim lifted down his prize find. "It's a Russian seaman's cap. See the Russian writing inside? It must have blown off one of those fellows on the fishing ships that come so close to shore."

"Oh!" cried Skip. "I wish I could find something that good!" He grabbed the cap and stuck it on his head. Rolling his eyes, he strutted up and down. Corky and Jim and Nogs laughed until they fell onto the bed and gasped for breath.

"I didn't know you could be so funny!" chuckled Corky. "Do it again!"

A door slammed.

"That must be Pop!" Jim tore into the living room to greet a square-jawed, jolly man. "Pop, did you hear the storm warnings on your car radio? Oh, this is Corky, and this is Skip. You know Nogs."

"Hello, boys. Yes, I did hear. Let her howl! We're safe and warm inside. And, if my nose tells me right, it's pot roast for dinner!"

Good smells were coming from the kitchen. Everyone sat down at the table in the corner of the living room. Mr. Mahony began to pass out plates of roast and vegetables.

"The limit tonight is five helpings, Nogs," he joked. Nogs's enormous appetite had astonished Corky's family too. Every time he came to spend the night with Corky, Mom just laughed and cooked extra-big amounts of everything.

"Joe, the baby refused her last bottle," worried Mrs. Mahony. "I think she's sick."

"Take her temperature after dinner," Mr. Mahony advised. "Corky Downs, I want to hear about your famous snake! The way Jim talks . . ."

Should he run into the bedroom and get the bag right this minute? Wouldn't the Mahonys and Skip be surprised to find that Sam was right here on the houseboat! But he'd better not tell yet.

Jancie wailed from her crib. Mrs. Mahony went over to check her. She came back to the table frowning. "Joe, come see. She's burning with fever. Babies come down with things so suddenly! She was bundled up quite warmly when I went to pick the children up at school."

"Now, dear," soothed Jim's father. "Calm down. Let's call Dr. Field and ask his advice. We don't want to drive into the office on this kind of night unless it is absolutely necessary."

"You take care of Jancie, Mom. We'll do the dishes," said Jim.

Mrs. Mahony hesitated. "Not more than two can squeeze into that galley."

"Corky, you and Skip can play a round of parcheesi with me while Jim and Nogs tackle the dishes," said Mr. Mahony.

The storm lashed angrily at the windows. Sitting cross-legged on the carpet, Corky could feel the boat rock. Here inside everything was safe and warm and cozy.

After the first game, Mr. Mahony got up and went to the telephone. In a few minutes he went out to the kitchen to talk with Jim.

"Could you boys stay out of mischief while your mother and I drive Jancie to the doctor's office? Her fever is high. Dr. Field wants to check her this evening."

"Sure, Pop!" Jim's face looked very solemn. "We won't horse around, will we, fellows?"

"Don't worry! We'll be all right!" they promised.

"Stay inside," warned Mrs. Mahony. "No need to go out on deck to watch the storm, hear? I hate to leave you alone, but it can't be helped. If you need an adult, phone Mr. Fairly's houseboat. I saw his light on."

Jim stood straight and tall by his mother. He put an arm around her plump middle and kissed her cheek. Then he parted the blankets and took a worried peek at Jancie. The baby's cheeks and forehead were fiery red.

When the Mahonys opened the door, the boys could see the lights of the other houseboats shining into the dark, wet night. After they had gone, nobody felt like talking.

At last, Jim said, "Want to play another game?"

"Naw, let's turn out the lights and read a ghost story from Corky's book."

"Let's don't!" said Skip.

"Let's think of something else," agreed Corky.

"I know," said Jim. "Have any of you ever sent a note off inside a bottle?" He grinned at the queer looks on their faces. "Shucks, you don't just read about it in books. You can really do it!"

"You're kidding!"

"No, I've done it myself. I sent four bottles with notes and my name and address. I got letters back from two people. One note only got to Astoria on the coast. But the other went as far as Hawaii. I'll show you." Jim disappeared into his bedroom. He came back and passed an envelope around.

"We could each send our own bottle!" said Corky.

Jim looked for pencils and papers and empty bottles. After a long time he found four bottles with tight lids—an old vitamin-pill bottle, an empty mustard jar, and two baby-food jars.

They chewed the ends of their pencils, thinking up what to say.

"My name is Corky Downs. I have a pet snake named Sam."

"My name is Skip. I am spending the night on my friend's houseboat."

"My name is Nogs. We are having a bad storm tonight."

"My name is Jim. I live on a houseboat. Please write."

"We'll throw them out my bedroom window," Jim said after they put addresses on the notes. "Mom and Dad didn't say anything about windows."

Rainwater blew in and soaked them. The wind howled. Gusts of air cut into the warmth of the tiny bedroom. They tossed the bottles. Jim banged the window shut.

"Did you see our deck? The water is washing over it!"

"Feel the boat sway!" cried Nogs. There was a loud crack. The houseboat lurched again. "Maybe we're breaking loose!"

"Don't be silly. Pop keeps everything in good repair."

"Houseboats do break loose, though," said Skip. "I read it in the newspaper. I'm scared! Besides, I'm gonna be—" He fled into the bathroom. When he returned, his face was as white as paste. "I'm seasick," he said miserably.

Corky felt sorry for him. He too was beginning to have a

squeamish feeling from the rocking of the boat.

"Your freckles are sticking out, Corky," began Nogs. Just then every light on the boat winked off.

Now what? No lights!

Corky groped around the bed in the pitch-black room. His hands grasped Nogs's shoulders. That small person giggled wildly.

"Oh, shut up!" muttered Corky. "I need my flashlight! Hurry!"

Jim raised the window. "Lean out to get sick. There's so much water on deck it'll wash right into the river."

"Ooooh!" moaned Corky when he was through. "I didn't know you got seasick on houseboats!"

Jim had disappeared. Now he called from the living room, "Our phone's dead. We *are* in a pickle! Mom and Pop can't reach us!"

He found his father's large battery torch. It flickered on his excited face. "They've probably been trying to call!"

A mighty cracking sound drowned out his voice. The boat lurched violently. Two cups and saucers slid from the counter and crashed on the floor. The boys tumbled like bowling pins.

"Hey, we're moving!" hollered Corky. "Jim! Jim! I'm sure this boat is moving!"

Jim was as alarmed as the rest of them. He hurried into the living room cupboard to get life jackets, banging into furniture as he went. He tossed the jackets to the boys and shouted above the din, "Put them on! Quick! The houseboat is loose from the mooring! The cable must have broken! Hang on! Don't panic! One of the Coast Guard boats will rescue us pretty quick."

"Will we smash? Will we get carried out into the ocean?" Nogs's eyes sparked. He did not seem to be scared at all. But Skip, forgetting about his queasy stomach, seemed crazy.

"Stop the boat! Stop the boat! I don't want to drown! I'm —I'm sc-scared; *Eeeeeeeeeeeooweeeeeeee!*"

His piercing scream was too much for Corky. With one hand he hung on to a built-in cupboard shelf. With the other he whammed Skip across the face. It was a mighty smack.

"Stop, Skip!"

For weeks he'd been waiting for a chance to whale the pants off Skip Lacey. But now that he'd cracked him, he only felt sorry for him!

"Skip," he said more kindly, "you kneel on the couch and pull up the shades so you can keep watch for the Coast Guard boat."

"That's right, Corky," said Jim. "They get to the spot fast in emergencies. You watch from the window in the kitchen door. And, Nogs, you take my bedroom window. I'll be in the folks' room. Gosh, this boat is tilting, so I guess we'll have to crawl on the floor!"

"I don't think we've sprung any leaks," he called in a few minutes. "We'd better be on the lookout for a log jam, though. We wouldn't want to ram into something like that." He was trying to sound cheerful, but his voice was shaky.

Hours passed. Or was it only minutes? The boat was heavy, but the current seemed to carry it swiftly.

What about Mom and Dad? Were they asleep? Or were they up watching the late news on TV? Pictures of the storm might be flashed on the local report. And Sam . . . curled under his flowerpot . . . but, wait, Sam was here!

"Sam!" yelled Corky. "I forgot about you!"

"He's safe," called Nogs. "His bag slid down under Jim's bed, but he isn't hurt. I felt his muscles through the cloth."

If Skip heard, he said nothing. He was too worried.

If only Corky could be sure Nogs was right! But he didn't dare leave his post at the window to check.

Jim called, "Any sign of the Coast Guard boat? I bet my parents are worrying themselves sick!"

"The wind seems to be letting up," reported Corky. "The boat isn't moving so fast anymore. Hey, look what's happening!"

The houseboat tilted and scraped. With a sudden bump-bump that landed them all on the floor again, it came to a standstill.

"Land!" shouted Skip.

"I think we've run aground on that little island out in the middle of the river," hollered Jim. "The one they call Sandy Point. Are we lucky! I say, are we ever lucky!"

"I always wanted to get shipwrecked!" Skip was feeling braver now that they seemed to be safe. He laughed sheepishly. "Not killed, just shipwrecked."

By the light of the battery torch, they met in the middle of the living room floor and banged each other joyfully on the shoulders, bumping life jackets.

"What next?" Jim was thoughtful. "I guess we *can't* do anything but wait for someone to find us."

"We could flash a signal with your father's torch," suggested Skip.

"Skip, that's a great idea!" shouted Jim. "The storm is beginning to let up. They're sure to see it."

"Let's have a party while we wait," said Nogs. "Your mother told us she made cinnamon buns."

Jim got them from the breadbox. "There's six apiece. If anyone feels too seasick to eat his, I can manage a few extra."

"Goody," said Nogs. " So can I."

"I feel fine now." Corky reached for a bun. Pretty soon, when the boys were helping themselves to thirds and fourths, he went into Jim's bedroom and closed the door to check on Sam.

The snake acted as if nothing had happened. He wrapped himself around Corky's arm and flicked his tongue out.

"Probably you're the only snake in the whole United States who's been shipwrecked!" said Corky.

Now and then, Jim flashed an SOS signal with the torch. Suddenly he put a finger to his lips and flashed again. "I hear something!"

"Everybody safe?" called a voice.

"Corky, Jim, Nogs, Skip!" called another voice.

"It's Mr. Fairly and Pop!" cried Jim. "They must be on the Coast Guard boat! We're getting rescued!"

"Thank God you're safe! We'll wire shore immediately," said Mr. Fairly as the boys climbed into the boat.

"Jim, your mother has been crying her eyes out!" declared Mr. Mahony. He kept mussing the boys' hair and patting their shoulders.

"And Jancie?"

"She has a bad case of flu. They kept her overnight at the hospital."

"As a volunteer member of the river patrol," said Mr. Fairly, "I'd like to congratulate you boys for keeping your heads. You were wise to stay inside. And it certainly was a good move to think of signaling!"

"That was Skip's idea," said Corky.

In the dark, Skip jostled Corky's shoulder

Corky jostled back. "I'm sorry I slapped that hard."

"Forget it," muttered Skip. "I was a dumbbell to screech."

Mr. Fairly had slickers for them to put on. The wind blew hard. The water was choppy and the boat ride was rough. But the rain no longer drove down in torrents.

"I wonder if the D.C. shack blew down," whispered Jim. "We'd better make tracks over there first thing in the morning to see."

"We'll spend the rest of the night at your grandmother's house, Jim. The houseboat will have to be towed back to the moorage and repaired," said Mr. Mahony. "Corky, would your folks be able to put Nogs up for the night if we take Skip along with us?"

"Sure," said Corky. "Nogs has stayed at our house lots of times." He was excited about telling Mom and Dad this new adventure. But he remembered to hide Sam's bag under his jacket. On top of greeting a shipwrecked son, the extra shock of seeing Sam would never do.

Mom greeted them, teary-eyed. Dad said gruffly, "How about some cocoa while you tell us about it, son?" Like the other men, when he heard how the boys had kept control of the situation, he looked proud.

Nogs and Corky got ready for bed.

"You take the cot this time," Corky told him. "I'm so

tired, I could sleep on a pile of thistles." He spread out his sleeping bag and climbed in. After a minute he got out again and found Sam's bag, which he set beside his pillow.

"It was fun tonight," murmured Nogs, half asleep.

"Yes," said Corky. "And you know something? Skip isn't half so bad. Nogs, tomorrow let's go look at our clubhouse. Jim's right. It might have blown away!"

CHAPTER 8

MYSTERIOUS CLUES

Not a splinter of the old shack had been harmed by wind and rain.

"My roof patches held!" Jim announced with glee. He had climbed up to inspect them, first thing.

But the storm had left all kinds of debris in its wake. For a long time after that, the D.C.s added new treasures to their already loaded shelves.

"We've got to sort some of this stuff out," said Corky. Hands on his hips, he surveyed the overflowing shelves. "The wasp's nest is good enough to keep. And this last skin that Sam shed is interesting. And, Jim, your agates. And the crow's nest and the cocoons. And the deer antlers. But, Nogs, that jar of worms has got to go!"

"Throw away something of your own," said Nogs. "Those are my pets. I guess earthworms are just as good to study as snakes."

"I'll take part of my rock collection home," said Jim. "And we'll give Pauline's blue-jay feathers back to her, and her fossils. She isn't in this club anymore."

"I still don't see why she got so huffy," said Nogs.

"I think she's jealous because Sam made me famous around school," said Corky. "Pauline wants to be the one everyone talks about. She doesn't like it when someone else gets to be it."

"Since she doesn't come anymore, could we invite Skip to be a D.C.?" Jim stared at the cocoon he was holding, not sure what the others would say.

"Sure!"

"He's some clown when you get to know him!"

"He might eat a lot though," said Nogs. Jim silenced him with a look that meant, Maybe he's kind of fat, but look how much you eat yourself!

Skip was delighted to be asked to join. In fact, he was the one who plunged the D.C.s into a new and mysterious adventure.

It happened this way.

The strong light bulb Bob Elton had advised Corky to put over Sam's cage was a big help. But now that Sam's body was being kept at the right temperature, he needed two or three mice a month to keep him happy.

Miss Puckett had connections with a laboratory. What a relief! For a while it looked as if Sam could have a proper dinner every week!

But after his first laboratory-mouse dinner, the snake refused to eat any more.

"Your snake is not so dumb after all, Benjamin," said Miss Puckett. "Those lab mice may have been treated with chemicals for experiments. They look fine, but Sam probably knows they are different."

"Oh, pooh!" said Corky. "Now I'll have to start saving

my allowance again. Boy, are pet-store mice expensive!"

"Wouldn't he eat dead ones?" asked Nogs. "I'm sure I could get some. My brother sets traps to catch the ones that nest inside our walls."

"No, he won't eat dead mice. But traps! Maybe I could make a trap for live mice in Shop! We could try catching field mice down near our shack."

Cold, rainy, end-of-November weather had come. The Grow students spent most afternoons working inside the shop. Already they had built the sides of a greenhouse. These were leaning against the shop wall. Some boys were making lamps and other things to sell at the May Carnival. Others were working on their own projects.

You could build practically anything in Mr. Fairly's shop class! Anything at all!

When Mike asked if he might start on a picnic table, Mr. Fairly said, "Yes, if your father will pay for the lumber."

When Fred asked if he could make an indoor slide to use on his basement steps, the instructor laughed and said, "Sure, as long as we have room to store the pieces."

He listened to Corky's plan for a trap for live mice. He did not say, "Why?" or "That won't work." He said, "By George, try it and see!"

When he finished the trap, Corky set it near the shack and put fresh bait in it every day. But each time he checked, the story was the same. No sign of nibbled cheese. Not a speck of mouse dirt!

Maybe field mice didn't eat cheese. He tried raw bacon. He tried buttered toast. Surely there must be a hungry mouse someplace!

When Skip joined the club and saw the trap, he said,

"I'll make two more. If we set three, we might catch a mouse in one."

In a week he made two very good mousetraps.

"Wow!" said Corky. "It took me over two weeks to make one trap. You're quick!"

Skip did not mind making traps. But one thing about the D.C. shack did bother him. The snakes! The jar of worms, the frogs, Toby the lizard, did not scare him. But the garter snakes and the red racer did.

The worst was when Corky sneaked Sam out of his cage in the schoolroom and over to the shack for a visit. At the sight of the collecting bag Skip grew pale.

"You won't take him out while I'm here, will you?" he said.

"You go outside," Corky argued. "Just for a few minutes. This is the only time I get to visit with Sam. Besides, he's our mascot. You can't be afraid of the mascot of your own club!"

"Do what I did," Nogs told Skip one day. "Sam isn't so scary when his tongue isn't flicking at you. When he's halfway under the flowerpot, reach out and touch his tail. After a while you can pet him while Corky is holding him good and tight."

"Yes," agreed Jim. "You'll get to be such good friends you'll be able to put him around your neck. Like this!"

Skip groaned as Jim grabbed the big snake and wound him around his neck. "Oh! Do I have to?"

"Yes," Corky said. "I know what! Clubs have initiation ceremonies. We'll start today and think of things for us all to do. None of us ever did get initiated into this club. Learning how to hold Sam will be one of the things."

"We could each find something special for our discovery shelf," said Nogs. He began making a list in the back of his school notebook.

"Every member must do some work on the shack," put in Jim.

"Let's say we each have to help a creature in distress," said Skip.

"Good!" said Corky. "When shall we have our initiation ceremony?"

"I think it would be fun to wait a while," said Skip. The others knew he probably wanted time to get used to the snakes. "How about the end of May? Carnival time?" To make up for being a scaredy, he added, "How about if I paint the inside of this place? We've got lots of leftover paint in our garage."

"Sure! You could do it crazy—one white wall, one black, one red . . ."

Skip went over to check a wall. Nogs started to make an initiation chart. Corky went to work cleaning the sides of his garter-snake cage. Jim kept Sam dangling around his neck while Corky worked.

Somebody sneezed.

"*Gesundheit!*" said Corky without turning around.

There was another sneeze, and another.

"*Gesundheit!* Who's doing that?"

"I didn't sneeze." Nogs looked up, startled.

"Me either!"

"Or me!"

"Oh, golly!" Jim turned around, his eyes wide. "Shhhh!"

He tiptoed to the window and peered out. The other D.C.s held their breath.

"No one in sight!"

"But I heard a sneeze!" said Corky. "Nogs, are you positive you didn't sneeze?"

"I ought to know if I sneezed or not!"

We've never seen anybody around here," said Jim.

"How about Pauline?" asked Corky.

"I'm going to go look." Skip sounded braver than he felt.

He left.

Minutes passed. "For goodness' sakes," grumbled Nogs. "What's happened to him?"

"I hope it wasn't a real tramp," worried Corky. "One of us should have gone with him."

They heard Skip whistle, and they rushed outside into the raw and misty dusk.

"Look!" cried Skip. "A footprint!"

They all stared at the large, clear footprint in the mud.

"One print," said Corky. "Whoever made it must have walked through the weeds." The print headed toward the river.

"That isn't a girl's footprint either!" exclaimed Jim. "It looks like a man's boot. I wonder if it was the owner of the shack."

"We aren't hurting anything. In fact, we're fixing this place up better than when we found it," said Nogs. "But we'll have to keep a sharp lookout from now on."

"We've never seen a No Trespassing sign," said Corky.

"If somebody asks us to leave, I guess we'll have to clear out," said Skip.

It was getting late. Nogs sighed. "I hope no owner turns up until after Christmas vacation. I was planning to spend

a lot of time down here. There isn't much to do where I live and this is so much fun!"

He started off on his long cold trek through the rain.

"I wish he lived closer," said Corky. He shivered. Nogs would be soaked by the time he reached home. "You fellows go on. I'll lock up."

He locked up. Then he pushed through the brush, wiping rain out of his eyes. He jogged down the road along the riverfront. The small, woodsy lot the shack was on stretched no longer than a city block. As Corky got to the end of it, he stood at the side of the road, shocked.

Someone was singing in the rain!

Was he hearing things? It was very dark now. The evening traffic had thinned out. It must be late. One part of him cried out, Go home to dinner! The other part of him shouted, Stay and see!

He cupped his hand to his ear, but heard nothing more. His eyes, growing used to the dark, saw nothing but trees and shrubs, ghostly shadows in the blackness.

It *was* a voice, Corky told himself. I know it was. The D.C.s probably won't believe me. But it was a voice!

CHAPTER 9

A CHANGE OF PLANS

"I thought *I* heard a girl singing," Skip said. "When I went outside and saw that footprint. I didn't want to say anything because . . . just because."

"I know how you feel," Corky told him.

"But the print was from a man's boot and it was a *girl's* voice."

"There must have been two people spying on us."

Nogs sneezed. "There," joked Corky. "I did hear a sneeze!"

"I cod a code," Nogs said thickly. He sneezed again and snuffled. "Bill wanted be to stay hobe today."

He looked chalky white. His lunch sandwich was not touched. When Nogs was not hungry, something was wrong!

The D.C.s had crowded to the end of a lunch table so that classmates would not listen to them.

"Lucky Christmas vacation begins the end of this week," said Jim. "We'll have time to hunt for more clues."

"You will, but not me." Corky looked mournful. "My

Idaho cousins are coming. I'll have to stick around home." The very thought of two small cousins spending a whole vacation filled him with gloom.

There was another bothersome thing. What about Sam?

Sam couldn't be left at school for two weeks. Probably nothing bad would happen. But the heat would be turned low. And suppose his water dish got dry. Or suppose he got stuck, silly snake, trying to crawl through the tiny hole in the top of his flowerpot.

"You leaving Sam in school?"

Corky jumped. Nogs must be a mind reader!

"I dunno. I *can't* take him home. And the D.C. shack is too cold except for short visits."

"Each of us could take hib hobe for three days." Nobs grinned at Skip's look of horror.

But then Skip said bravely, "I—let me have him first. I don't have to take him out or feed him, do I? I could put his cage in our basement. It might help me get used to him if I just look at him every day."

"How about your mother? Will she faint or scream?"

"She won't even see him," promised Skip. "He'll be hidden."

"Lacey, first three days. Mahony, the next three," said Jim. "My mother won't care if the cage is in sight as long as I don't unlock it. She laughed when I told her Sam was visiting us the night of the storm."

"Count be for the last four days," offered Nogs. He sneezed again.

"You fellows are swell!" said Corky. "I've got a small cage I can bring so we won't have to haul the big one around. It doesn't have a lock, but all you need to do is weight the lid with something heavy."

The days were full. Presents to finish in the shop, last minute errands to run for frantic parents, decorations to help put up, homework to finish. Not one D.C. found a spare minute to stop by the shack.

Nogs might have gone by, since he had no mother to make him wax floors or wash windows. But all week his cold kept him indoors. The last three days he did not come to school. He had no telephone. Corky worried about him.

On Friday at three thirty, the doors of the River School burst open. Down the steps rushed a mob of children, throwing winter caps in the air and shouting. Vacation had started!

Corky helped Skip smuggle Sam's smaller cage into his basement. Then he hurried back past the school toward home. Ten long, empty days ahead! Not even the idea of visiting cousins dampened his spirits. Streetlamps glowed in the dusk. Many people had put their trees up already. Colored lights sparkled through their front windows. There were outside Christmas lights too. One house had eight plywood reindeer and a Santa and sleigh prancing across its roof.

Pauline's parents had turned their garage into a manger. Real straw, life-size figures. Corky paused to look.

"Merry Christmas, Corky!" Pauline bounced down her back steps. She stood beside him, gazing at the manger scene. "We add something new each year. This time it's the biggest camel. Gee, Corky . . . I never told you but I—I'm sorry I stuck Sam in Carla's sweater pocket."

"*You did?*" Corky was flabbergasted. "Why?"

"To tease her. But I got busy with an art project and I

forgot to go back and take him out. You sounded so cross I was afraid to say anything. Anyway, I've told you now. I'm sorry!"

"That's O.K." said Corky. "Forget it." He grinned at Pauline. "Want to come back and be a D.C. again?"

Pauline nodded happily.

"Say, did you come spy on us?"

"I haven't been there since I quit. Honest, Cork."

He whistled softly. "Then it *was* somebody else! Pauline, I'll call you up tonight and tell you about it. I got to go. I promised Mom I'd clean my room this afternoon."

It wasn't a hard job, the room, because most of the collection had been moved to the shack. First Corky lay down on his stomach and dragged stuff out from under the bed. The dirty laundry he piled by the door. Aha! There was his long lost moccasin slipper! And his ballpoint pen. He lifted the overflowing trash basket, the books, the Monopoly game, and two empty pop bottles to the top of his table. Then he began to vacuum. Cousin Joe and little Peter would be spreading their sleeping bags on his floor. Better shove things around to make room.

Pretty soon he gathered the armful of laundry and went into the bathroom.

The telephone rang. Mom was answering it.

"Corky!" Mom came in. Turning, Corky saw that she looked worried. "I know you'll be disappointed. That was a call from Idaho. Grandma slipped on the ice. She broke her hip, so the cousins must stay home to take care of her."

Corky didn't actually feel too sorry. The corners of his mouth twitched.

"Sorry about Grandma," he said. "Worse luck!" Suddenly he *was* sorry too. Grandma was a great old girl, not a bit like Aunt Mildred. And Mom and Dad had been looking forward to this big Christmas get-together for weeks. Silver polished, windows gleaming, wreaths hanging, the biggest tree they'd bought in years.

The small cousins would have been somebody to talk to. And somebody was better than nobody. Now he still had nobody at all. Not even Sam.

"I was thinking," Mom went on in her soft, husky voice, "it isn't much fun to celebrate Christmas alone. We don't know anyone in Portland well enough to invite over. How about Bill and Nogs?"

Corky flung his arms around her. "You're the best!" he yelled. "You *are* the best!" He thought a minute and said, "Nogs is half sick with a cold. And they don't have a telephone. I have his address though."

"We'll drive over after dinner. Christmas is two days away, time to get a few small gifts . . ."

Corky wasn't listening. He was outside tearing around and around the house as if one of Mr. Scarborough's cats had turned into a tiger and was after him.

As soon as the dishes were cleared from the table, they took off with the Portland street map to find Nogs's house. Mr. Downs drove slowly. It was a part of the city unfamiliar to any of them.

"Kind of run down," he observed. "Why does Nogs take a bus to the River School? There must be a school closer to his house than that."

"His brother read about the new Grow Program in the newspaper. He got special permission for Nogs to change schools." As soon as the words popped out, Corky wished they hadn't. Dad was so quiet he was probably thinking of finding another school for Corky. He was always taking a crack at Mr. Mac's weird ideas.

Corky looked at the paper with Nogs's address. "That corner house must be it. The one with the cardboard on the front window."

He stood in the dingy yard. It was littered with paper. What was Mom thinking? She looked so—well, so *clean* in Nogs's yard. Her shoes polished, her makeup fresh and pretty, her hair neatly combed.

So far, she had never once objected to having Nogs come over to visit. But now that she was seeing where he lived, she might change her mind. It was an uncomfortable feeling, as if they'd finally discovered a secret Nogs had been trying to hide.

Bill answered their knock. He was a short, thin boy who looked like a high school senior instead of a garage mechanic. Behind him stood Nogs, his cheeks flushed with fever.

"We came to invite both of you to join us for Christmas dinner on Monday," said Mrs. Downs. "Bill, it would be our pleasure to have you. And I know it would make the day for Corky."

"It would be *our* pleasure, ma'am," Bill said gravely. "If Nogs is well enough by then, we'd be happy to accept. Could I call you from a pay phone on Sunday evening?"

Corky's glance took in the paper plate of beans sitting on a chair, and the torn quilt on the couch where Nogs had been lying with a book.

Mr. Downs spoke up. "Why don't you let Nogs spend his vacation with us?" he asked. "If we take him home tonight,

my wife can dose him up with cough syrup and hot soup, and the other things he needs for that cold."

As Nogs sneezed, Mom added, "Sure, Bill. He needs a day or two in bed. It will be more fun for him with Corky around."

Corky was surprised into silence. But Nogs, with an unexpected burst of energy, did a jig around the room. "Say yes, Bill! Please? Oh, boy! *Oh, boy!*"

He was so funny that everyone chuckled.

"It'll be like having a twin brother!" shouted Corky. "Please say yes, Bill, please!"

"And you can come over in time for a noon dinner on Christmas day," Mom told him.

By now both boys were running around the house as if the matter had been decided.

"Pajamas!" said Nogs.

"Blue jeans!" said Corky.

"Library book. It's a mystery!" shouted Nogs.

"Shoes . . . toothbrush . . . don't worry about clean shirts, Mom'll wash them . . ."

"He doesn't look too sick to me," laughed Bill. "But having him over at your place certainly would take a load off my mind."

As soon as they got home, Corky began dumping clothes out of one drawer into another.

"Whad are you doing?"

"You'll be here a week," said Corky. "You need some room for your duds, don't you?"

A little later he said, "You take the cot again. You're sick, you know." He settled down into his sleeping bag, and Nogs got into bed.

"Led's do somethig different every day of vacation!" he planned between sneezes. "One day we cad sell the rest of our school candy bars so we cad go on a great big trip in the spring. Ad another day we'll do nothing but hunt clues ad the shack. Say, Cork!" He sat up in bed and leaned over to punch Corky between the shoulder blades. "Whad aboud Sam? When my turn comes—"

"Pauline'll take him. She's back in the club. I'll explain tomorrow. I'm too sleepy now!"

Two days in bed, three hot meals a day, and plenty of cough syrup worked a speedy cure for Nogs.

"I know how to gargle to the tune of 'Jingle Bells'!" he boasted to Corky.

On Christmas morning the boys awoke at dawn. Nogs had already been in to see the tree before Corky unzipped his sleeping bag.

"My pile of gifts is as big as yours!" Nogs told him in surprise. "How did your mom and dad do that in two days?"

There was a skateboard for Corky and one for Nogs. There were airplane models, a new sweater for each, and books. Nogs had a pocketknife and Corky had a pair of field glasses.

"They are an excellent secondhand pair," Dad said. "We thought you might like to take up birds instead of snakes." He sounded half serious.

He seemed pleased with the inlaid checkerboard Corky had made for him in Shop. And Mom smoothed the waxed finish on her bookends and exclaimed, "They're lovely, Corky! Such fine work!"

Late in the morning, Bill arrived. He brought a *Hot Rod*

Magazine for each boy and a box of chocolates for Mr. and Mrs. Downs. There was a sweater waiting for him under the tree, like the one Nogs had received but four sizes larger.

"The magazines are kind of a joke," said Bill. His eyes twinkled. "Nogs, if you feel well enough to go outside, your present from me is on the porch."

Out rushed Nogs. He shouted so loud that everyone else ran to see if he'd fallen down the steps.

"A bike!" he yelled. "A bike! Gee whillikers, Bill!" His quick, happy look at Corky meant: No more hiking in the rain.

At dinner they stuffed themselves on turkey and dressing and cranberry sauce, mashed potatoes, salad, and two kinds of pie. Nobody counted Nogs's helpings. He ate on and on and on. Once he stopped long enough to tell Mrs. Downs she was a good cook. She smiled and filled his plate all over again.

"Corky," said his father while they waited for Nogs to finish, "there is one more gift that was too large to wrap. You've been so good about giving away your menagerie and keeping your room fixed up, we feel you deserve a real bed instead of that flimsy army cot. It's a double one. That way, you can invite friends to spend the night without bothering about sleeping bags."

Corky grinned. Now he could invite a boy or two any time—Jim, Roy, Skip. Looking across the table at Nogs, he knew in his heart who would come most often.

The boys left Bill and Mr. and Mrs. Downs having coffee in the living room. They tried out Nogs's bike. Corky rated it as good as his own.

"It was sure great of Bill to get it!" said Nogs. "He must have been saving for months!"

"Wait till I go get my bike," said Corky. "I'll race you over to Pauline's. She's going to be excited about our skate-boards. Let's get Jim and Skip, too, and have a Christmas meeting at the shack. Maybe we'll find more clues!"

CHAPTER 10

MORE TROUBLE FOR SAM

Several of the Christmas holidays dawned clear and bright. The D.C.s spent quite a bit of time hunting for clues. They found nothing. No more footprints, no voices, no sign of any stranger coming near the shack.

They gave up hunting for spies and went skateboarding. Everyone except Skip had a skateboard now, and Pauline lent him an old one to use. When she showed them how to do tricks, Skip turned out to be the fastest learner. That Skip!

"I got used to Sam too," he bragged. "I bet I could have kept him six or seven days in my basement without any trouble."

"Aw, that's because you didn't have to pick him up! You wait till our initiation!" said Nogs. He was beginning to be friends with Skip, but he liked to tease him.

"I have to watch my duck, Waddles," laughed Jim. "This morning he flew up on Sam's cage and nearly knocked the books off the top."

Corky groaned. "You be careful, Jim!" If only he could

have Sam home to watch and hold during vacation! His new binoculars were great but he wasn't about to study birds instead of reptiles. Why couldn't Dad get that through his head? And what would Mom say if she found he hadn't given away his menagerie after all, just parked it in a different place?

"It's your turn to start having Sam today," Jim told Pauline.

Pauline giggled. "I think I'm going to have to keep him under my bed. My bedspread will hide his cage all right. And nobody cleans the room except me. Can he live for a few days without any light, Corky?"

"Dumbbell! What do you think he did down in Skip's basement? Darkness puts him off his feed, that's all."

Corky left his skateboard at the shack and carted the snake cage over to the Tyler house. Pauline trailed behind. He waited while she went inside to make certain no one was around. In a few minutes, she whistled.

At the top of the stairs, Corky rested the cage on a bookshelf and lifted Sam out for a minute. "You pretty thing!" he said as he stroked his velvety skin. "Why don't people like snakes? What do they have against them?"

"Come on, Corky. I think Mom's over at the neighbor's having coffee. I don't know how she feels about snakes, but she's scared of mice, and I don't want to take any chances."

"That's exactly what I mean!" Corky said. "What's so bad about snakes?"

"I think they're gorgeous, especially Sam," said Pauline. "But hurry up and put him back so I can hide his cage!"

"Good-by, Sam!"

The next morning the boys awoke to the plink-plink of rain on the roof. Mrs. Downs insisted that they stay inside.

"Watch TV. Or finish your Christmas models," she said. "After a bad cold like that, Nogs should not run the risk of getting soaked."

"The shack is as dry as a bone!" Corky wanted to howl. But, of course, Mom did not know about the shack.

"Only two more days of vacation," said Nogs on Saturday. "The rain has stopped. Let's go get Pauline and Jim and Skip and think of something exciting to do."

Pauline's mother answered the door. "She has to spend the night in the hospital, boys. She slipped and broke her leg. She'll be home as soon as her cast gets dry."

Hospital? Cast? They could hardly believe their ears! How did it happen? That was the silliest part of all! Not twirling on ice skates down at the rink. Not swooshing downhill on her skateboard. No, indeed!

"Pauline," they reported to Skip and Jim, "slipped on her mother's freshly waxed kitchen floor. She broke two bones in her leg. She won't be allowed out on crutches for a month. Isn't that disgusting?"

Corky felt sorry for Pauline. But he felt sorrier for Sam. "I wish I could rescue him," he said. "This is terrible! Pauline won't be able to check him or give him clean water."

"He'll make out. You've told us lots of times—that's the best thing about having a snake for a pet," Jim reminded him. "They don't need much care."

But Corky worried. "What if her cat, Snow White, gets

into the room? She might hurt him with her claws!"

A telephone call cheered him up. Pauline was now home in her own bed. Her father had moved the extension phone so she could use it while she was laid up.

"Call me up every day," she told Corky gaily. "I want to know what's happening. I think Mom will let me have visitors by next Friday. My leg is so bad, they want me to stay really still."

"Don't you dare let that cat in while Sam is under your bed!" warned Corky. "Is there a way I could sneak him out and take him back to the classroom when school starts?"

At the other end of the line, Pauline burst into peals of laughter. "Don't worry! I've been extra careful about Snow White! Mom and Dad think I want her in here to keep me company. They can't understand why I keep asking them to take her away! Sam is where I can reach him, Corky, so I've had him up in bed for a visit. Had to stick him under the pillow when my big sister Sue brought my tray. Could I tell my little brother Ricky about him, do you think?"

"No, I *don't* think!" said Corky very crossly. "Ricky is only five."

Friday seemed a long way off. Especially after Nogs went back home on Sunday. The little bedroom at the side of the kitchen was empty. No Nogs. No Sam. Just Corky Downs lying awake worrying. Sooner or later, Snow White would find a way to get into Pauline's bedroom. And then what?

On Monday it was almost exciting to get back to school. Mr. Mac called an assembly to explain some new ideas.

"More field trips," he announced. "Try mixing a little

more. You fifth-graders take the third-graders with you on your next fossil-hunting trip. Fourth-graders, you find some project to share with the sixth-graders. If any of you don't like what you are studying, ask your teacher. Maybe she can change it. None of us should be afraid of *change.* Who says we must study the same things year after year?"

No need to say anything about the assembly at home. Dad seemed pleased enough with Corky's report-card grades. Maybe he had forgotten his idea of looking into other schools.

"We didn't sell any candy bars during vacation," Corky wrote in a note to Nogs. "The more we sell, the more field trips we get to go on."

Miss Puckett had said that they would save the big trip, the one to eastern Oregon, until school let out early in June. To Corky and Nogs, this trip sounded like more fun than any of the others. They made up for lost time and sold every candy bar in their cartons.

"My arms ache from carrying that box!" groaned Corky at the end of the week.

"Never mind," said Nogs. "I've got seven dollars and forty-five cents." He turned it over to Jim, who was the class treasurer.

"Here's my six twenty," reported Skip.

"Here's my six fifty-five," said Corky. "I'm not selling any from my next carton today, because Pauline's mother says I can visit her. First thing I'm going to do is—"

"Get Sam!" shouted a chorus of voices.

Mrs. Tyler was a fluttery, bustly mother. Just the type, thought Corky, to get hysterical over snakes. He wanted to greet Sam almost more than he wanted to visit with

Pauline. But Mrs. Tyler simply would not leave them alone. First she followed Corky upstairs to make sure there would be a chair for him. She asked him not to jiggle the bed and then left. Corky was just setting up the chessmen so he could teach Pauline how to play chess when Mrs. Tyler came back to ask questions.

"Are they hand-carved? Wood or ivory?"

"Plastic," said Corky. He wished she would go away.

She left, but before he could get down on his hands and knees to find Sam's cage, she came back with a plate of cookies and three plates of ice cream.

"Mind if I join you?" she asked pleasantly. "I've been ironing for two solid hours. I'd enjoy a rest."

To tell the truth, she was very nice. The cookies and ice cream tasted so good that it was easy for Corky to forgive her. Imagine how Mom would feel if *he* broke *his* leg on *her* kitchen floor!

Pauline knew what he was thinking about. She shot him a mischievous look. At last her mother left them to finish their game in peace. Corky dropped to the floor.

There was a muffled roar of distress. "Oh, murder! The book got knocked off! Sam's missing!"

"No!" cried Pauline.

"Yes!"

She rolled to the edge of her bed and hung over as far as she could go without falling out. "Lemme look. Snow White must have been in when I wasn't looking. Or maybe it happened when Dad rolled my bed over closer to the window. Golly, I'm sorry, Corky!"

"I should have known better," he said in misery. "He needs to be in a cage that has a lock."

"Corky! Look, there's sort of a humpy shadow over there in the corner. No, *there*, at the other end of the bed. Is that him?"

"Yes!" cried Corky, relieved. "Hang on and I'll get him!"

Pauline teetered on the edge of her bed. She moved her good leg to keep her balance. Cocoa cups, tray, chessboard and chessmen crashed to the floor.

"Merciful goodness!" Mrs. Tyler dashed upstairs and into the room. "Darling, whatever are you *doing?* Get back under the covers this minute! Corky, I believe you've been here long enough. Yes, yes, child, you can come again. But wait until Monday, please. This has been quite enough excitement for one day!"

Monday! That was two days away, and Sam was loose!

"Make them keep your bedroom door closed," he whispered to Pauline before he got hustled down the stairs and out the front door with his box of chessmen. "Tell them you have a headache. Tell them anything. But make them keep the door shut!"

Brother, was this a real mess! What could he do now?

The thought of poor Sam, loose inside a house where the family pet was a cat, made Corky want to throw up. At supper he played with his food. He couldn't swallow a mouthful.

"You must be coming down with something," worried his mother. "Tsk, tsk."

About nine o'clock Pauline called up. As soon as he got on the line, she giggled so hard she couldn't talk.

"Oh, shut up! It isn't funny!"

"It is too!" she told him. "You don't know what's happened. Mom lets Ricky go as far as the variety shop at the end of our block. I gave him my allowance and asked him to buy me a mouse to keep me company."

Corky moaned. "Don't complicate things!"

"I was planning to lean over and pull out Sam's flowerpot to make it into a kind of a mouse cage. I was going to tape the broken place at the bottom and leave a slit so Sam could slide through, but not a mouse."

"Don't do it!" begged Corky. "Mice can get in and out of tiny holes too. Snakes can't see so well and I don't have any idea whether Sam could *smell* a mouse at a distance. Especially if the mouse was inside a flowerpot."

"I was going to do it," went on Pauline, going off in another gale of laughter. "Ha, ha, ha, ha . . . I was about to try it and the mouse got loose. So, now there is a mouse *and* a snake—"

"Pauline Tyler!" exclaimed Corky. "If you let Snow White in your room to catch that mouse, my snake might wrap himself around her neck and choke her!"

This was not true. Snow White was such a strong, big cat that she might hurt the snake with her sharp teeth or claws. But he wanted to make Pauline worry. The dumb girl thought the whole thing was a joke!

"Remember," he said. "There's no telling what a corn snake might do to a cat! I'll bring over my new field glasses so you can look for Sam."

His words quieted Pauline. She got off the phone quickly to make sure Ricky had closed her bedroom door tight.

Chapter 11

THE RESCUE

When Corky stopped by to leave his binoculars (Dad called them "bird glasses") for Pauline, Mrs. Tyler looked puzzled.

"In bed?"

"Sure," said Corky. "She can put toast crumbs along her windowsill and watch the birds feeding."

There was a long weekend to wait before he could see Pauline again. In the meantime, a strange thing happened. It snowed!

What a surprise to wake up on Monday morning to a white world! The traffic and footstep noises were muffled! Corky jumped out of bed and ran to the window. Maybe there would be enough snow for sledding!

"Isn't this great?" shouted Jim when Corky came across the playground. "We hardly ever get more than a smidgen of snow in Portland!"

"Oh, boy!" Nogs skidded to a halt on the slippery white stuff. "We haven't had this much snow for four years! Maybe the school will have to shut down."

"Fat chance!" said Corky. It was fun to see some snow. But he was so worried about Sam that it was hard to be happy.

That afternoon he hurried over to Pauline's. She saw him coming and knocked on her window. She was yelling something. He could not tell what she was trying to say.

She waved to him and managed to raise her window partway.

"Mom is out doing errands. That means you can't come in," she called. "But I've thought of something new."

She began to let down a two-pound coffee can with a string tied securely around its middle. "Fill it with snowballs," she ordered.

"For Pete's sake! First tell me if you caught Sam!"

"How could I? But I did keep the door closed the whole time. And Snow White got in through the window last night and caught the mouse."

Corky looked unhappy. "If the cat got in, how do you know the snake didn't get *out*? Sam can climb!"

"For Pete's sake, yourself! What snake would want to go out into a cold, dark, snowy night? Please send some snowballs up in the can, Corky. The only time I've gotten to play in the snow was last year when Dad took me up into the mountains. And now this stupid leg is keeping me in!"

Corky scooped up some snow. Four snowballs fitted into the coffee can quite nicely. "Haul her up!"

"Now another load."

"What are you going to do with them? Your mother will bawl you out."

"She won't be back for an hour or so. Our snowball fight will be over before she gets here." Pauline giggled so happily that Corky sent up five more loads of snowballs. She seemed to be piling them on her windowsill and on her lunch tray.

"Ricky's a good kid," she called. "When I asked him to bring the sponge mop, he never said 'boo.' Ready?"

Corky had made another pile of ammunition for himself. Now he fired. Zing! And another . . . zing!

Pauline tossed three down. One hit him on the elbow. "Ho! Better luck next time!"

With perfect aim, he threw five more through the window. A snowball of Pauline's caught him squarely in the face. His nose began to bleed. The enemy above paused to give him time to doctor his wounds.

"Wow!" He rubbed his bleeding nose with a handful of snow. Then he called in a worried voice, "Pauline, get Ricky to hide the snowballs! Miss Puckett's car has turned down your street and, yes, it looks as if she's coming to visit you!"

Quickly Pauline dumped the rest of her ammunition out of the window. Corky could hear her asking Ricky to mop up the puddles. He stood at the side of the house finishing his own mop-up job.

Miss Puckett's car door opened and out she stepped.

"Why, hello, Benjamin! Is Pauline able to have visitors?"

"Hullo, Miss Puckett. Her mother is gone, but I'm sure it's O.K. if you go in," he said politely. "She gets so lonely that we were just calling back and forth through her window."

He wondered if he'd gotten all the blood wiped off his chin. Behind him, the window slammed shut.

"Give her a call at the foot of the stairs. She saw your

car, so she expects you to go on up to her bedroom. Uhhh
. . . Mrs. Tyler asked her to keep her bedroom door closed
tight . . ."

He did some fast thinking and followed the teacher into
the house. "Miss Puckett, I don't think Mrs. Tyler would
mind me visiting too, as long as another grown-up is here."

He tried to picture what the bedroom might look like
with puddles of melting snow.

He glanced around the room. No puddles, no squishy
bits of snow! Pauline's dancing eyes met his, and he turned
away.

Her blanket looked damp in one corner. When he sat
down on her desk chair, his eyes caught a forgotten snowball under the bed. But Ricky had done a great job of mop-
ping up in a hurry!

The teacher was showing Pauline a stack of library books
and a carton full of felt pieces, drawing paper, and paste.

"You can begin making little items to sell at the Carnival," she suggested.

"Thank you so much, Miss Puckett," said Pauline in a
sweet tone of voice. "I've been bored stiff lying still like
this!" When Miss Puckett's back was turned, she stuck out
her tongue at Corky.

"I take lots of naps," she added. "While Ricky is down
in the playroom watching TV. That's where he is now."
She glared over at Corky. "I sent him down to empty a
wastebasket. I suppose the naughty boy stayed to watch
cartoons!"

"Urrruff!" said Corky in a kind of cough. Ricky was probably out in the backyard right now, emptying out the
slush.

"Hurruf!" This time it sounded like a queer mixture of cough and sneeze. He'd just noticed Sam!

The snake was stretched out along the curtain rod of the window behind Pauline's bed. No wonder she had not been able to see him with the field glasses! Her curtains were brown-and-orange plaid. Sam's colors blended with them. How long had he been there? A few minutes? A day? And how had he climbed that high? Could a snake crawl up a curtain without slipping to the floor? Maybe Sam had journeyed up the pole of Pauline's study lamp and then over onto the curtain rod!

Should he tell Miss Puckett? The teacher was a good egg. Together they could get Sam back into his cage. Then Pauline's mother would never know.

"Many other people have been absent from school too," said Miss Puckett, trying to strike up an interesting conversation. "Not only pupils. Miss White has had flu. And Noah, the janitor, has had a bad case of pneumonia. I understand he won't be able to work for over a month."

When Corky gazed upward at Sam again, he yelped out loud without stopping to think, "He's shedding, that's what he's doing!"

"My stars!" exclaimed Miss Puckett. "How did your pet get up there?"

Pauline was so excited she pounded her pillow. She managed to twist herself carefully around in bed so that she could watch Sam too. "I knew we'd find him! How exciting! I've never seen a snake shed before and he's doing it right here in my own bedroom!"

"Most people never get to see such a thing," agreed Miss Puckett. "Snakes like privacy when they shed. See how he is wriggling in order to get out of that old skin. He turns it inside out. If he's lucky, it will come off in one piece like a suit of clothes."

"Sometimes he runs into trouble and has to shed it by bits," Corky told her, entranced. *He* had never watched Sam shed his skin either. It was almost worth all the worry he'd been through. "He seems to be rubbing himself along the rough side of the curtain rod to get it loose. Snakes start shedding at their head, don't they?"

"That is right, Benjamin. Sometimes the caps of skin covering their eyes do not get peeled off. They build up into a thick layer and—if the snake is living in captivity— a veterinarian or a herpetologist must remove the layers surgically. I've watched my father do it."

"Look, he's resting!" said Pauline. "Miss Puckett, what would happen if we helped him get out of his old skin?"

"I believe it would injure him badly, Pauline, so that he might not recover. He must go through the entire process alone. See, he is rubbing it again. Benjamin, perhaps you could make a report on this. The class would find it interesting to hear, from firsthand experience, how a snake does this!"

"I thought he was pretty before, but his new colors are so much brighter!" said Pauline.

"Yoo-hoo!" called a voice from the stairs. "Dearie, do you have visitors up there?"

"It's Mother! She's coming up!"

The bedroom door flew open and in walked Mrs. Tyler. "I *thought* I recognized your voice, Miss Puckett! How wonderful of you to visit Pauline! The child does get bored spending all this time in bed. And lovely of you to come too, Corky. Would everyone like some ginger ale and cupcakes? Where is Ricky—in the playroom?"

Her high heels clicked down the stairs. Corky whispered hoarsely, "Couldn't we let him finish shedding inside his cage?"

"No." Miss Puckett was firm. "Let me handle this. Pauline, are you absolutely certain your mother is afraid of snakes?"

Pauline thought a minute. "No. But she's scared to death of mice. Live ones, anyway. So she probably isn't too fond of other wiggly things."

Eyes glued to the curtain rod, they watched Sam move out of the last bit of old skin. He lay stretched along the top of the curtain in glistening beauty.

"Now!" cried Corky softly, ready to pounce. But they could hear Mrs. Tyler clicking up the stairs again with the refreshments.

Unaware of the mysterious process taking place on top of the window behind her, she passed the plate of cupcakes, the glasses of ginger ale, the napkins.

"I must say, there is nothing more cheery than visitors."

Miss Puckett's mouth quivered. Corky looked down at his glass of ginger ale. Nobody else seemed eager to make conversation, so Mrs. Tyler went on. "Pauline tells me your main interest is science. I was a zoology major in college, myself." She laughed and added, "Nothing bothered me except the mice. I dissected frogs, snakes, cats . . ."

Pauline choked on a bite of cupcake. Her mother ran to get a glass of water, and Miss Puckett whacked her on the back. Corky's mouth hung open. *All this trouble for nothing!* Should they tell her, or should they keep quiet and wait?

Pauline, through with choking, lay back on her pillow and covered her face with her hands. Corky began to chuckle and so did Miss Puckett. Mrs. Tyler looked from one to another.

"This is so funny!" exclaimed the teacher. "Benjamin, you tell the story."

"It's this way," began Corky.

Before he finished, Mrs. Tyler was laughing too. "No wonder Pauline kept wanting her bedroom door shut!"

"I'd better take your snake home tonight," said Miss Puckett. "Tomorrow we'll lock him in his big cage in the classroom. He's had quite enough adventure for a while!"

Corky scuffled home through the snow still smiling. Mrs. Tyler hated mice but didn't mind snakes. And Mrs. Mahony did not mind either of them as long as they were inside a cage. And little Miss Puckett turned out to be willing to handle any pet, large or small. Mom thought mice were cute but could not stand reptiles. Oh, why couldn't Mom be the one who thought snakes were beautiful?

A note from Jim Mahony was waiting on his table in his bedroom. "More footprints today! Fresh ones!" So, for a while, he did not think about snakes. He thought about footprints. He would get up early so he could stop by the shack before school began.

CHAPTER 12

THIEF!

Drip-drip, drip-drip. Corky awoke to the sound of melting snow. Doggone it! No chance of finding footprints today. Just the same, he hustled through breakfast and stopped by the D.C. shack on the way to school.

Staring down at the sloppy mixture of mud and snow, he could find no clue.

That was the first thing that went wrong.

The second thing was the way Mr. Baker, the substitute janitor, acted so mean about Sam.

"You kids can dust that shelf yourself as long as the big snake is there," he growled.

"Pooh!" said Corky to Nogs. "He's not half as nice as Noah. Why, Noah isn't a bit afraid of Sam! Who does he think he is, anyway?"

The third and worst thing of all happened in the middle of English class. Jim Mahony raised his hand and waved it wildly.

"Miss Puckett, Miss Puckett! I had twelve dollars of candy money in my desk and it isn't there now! I—I meant to give it to you first thing this morning to go in the bank!"

"Calm down, Jim. Try to remember exactly what you did," she said. "Let me look. Perhaps it got stuck in a book or under some papers."

The rest of the class held their breath while the teacher helped Jim look again. The two of them removed every single thing from his desk. Pencils, papers, maps, books. The money was not there.

Miss Puckett unlocked the door of her supply cupboard. She checked the shelves. She made each pupil empty his desk.

"I am not accusing any of you of stealing," she explained. "It is a possibility I don't like to think of. Perhaps the money did get mislaid. If Jim was in a big hurry last night, he might have lifted the lid of the wrong desk."

"No," said Jim. "It was here in an envelope in my own desk. I should have known better than to leave it at school all night."

The classroom was full of serious faces. No joking or smiling. It had taken a long time to earn that money by selling candy bars.

"Who could have done it?" Jim asked the rest of the D.C.s at lunchtime. They were all asking the same question. Who? *Who?*

All the time Corky was in Grow he kept wondering who was mean enough to steal money out of a boy's desk. Would they have to cancel the class trip to eastern Oregon?

Today the boys were finishing the big arches for the greenhouse. Mr. Fairly wanted to be able to put the greenhouse up in March. One group of boys checked and listed every piece. Others sanded some of the parts. Some took care of the varnishing. Some wrote down measurements for the amount of plastic needed for the outside. While they worked, everyone talked about the theft.

"Money has been missing from some of the desks in our room too," said a seventh-grader.

"The school bus gets here early," said Nogs suddenly. "I bet it's someone who rides the bus with me every day! But who?"

"Now we have two mysteries to solve," said Jim at the D.C. meeting later on. "The footprints in the snow, and this money business."

"The thing to do is to make a plan," said Corky. "We could each take turns hiding behind the bushes outside our classroom window. A thief might go back to check through the desks another time."

Nogs looked doubtful. "But suppose he tries a different classroom next time? I'm going to watch the kids on the bus every day. Maybe I'll see somebody sneak into school before the bell rings."

"Corky's right. If the thief heard that Jim is our class treasurer, he just might look in the same desk again." Skip's eyes were bright.

"Any sixth-grader knows Jim is treasurer," said Nogs.

What an awful idea! It was terrible to think somebody from Miss Puckett's room might turn out to be a thief.

"I know what!" shouted Jim. "We can ask Pauline to watch at her window every morning. And we *will* take turns hiding in the bushes, and the person who sees the robber can wave a white flag, and then Pauline can call the police!"

"I'll lend my field glasses to whoever is on guard behind

the bushes," said Corky. "The person on guard can pretend he's out watching for birds."

They decided that Nogs would have the first turn to be on duty.

The very next morning, Corky raced to school. Then, remembering that he did not want anyone to suspect anything, he sauntered by the bushes as if nobody were hiding there.

"Psst!" whispered Nogs. "Corky! There wasn't anybody around at all! Not a single person!"

But that day, more money was missing. This time it was Mike's lunch money.

"Only thirty-five cents," said Mike. "Anyone who bothers to take that change is a cheap skate!"

The next day, Jim took his turn behind the bushes. He too saw nobody.

"It's my turn tomorrow," Corky told Pauline when he stopped by her house. "I wish I'd have some luck. Mr. Mac said he'd wait only until next Monday before he called the police. He kind of hopes the person who did it will put the money back."

"I wish I could go to school!" Pauline thumped her cast against the end of the bed. Her eyes flashed. "I'd find that thief in a hurry!"

"Like fun you would! Us boys have been working hard on the case and we don't even have a clue yet," said Corky.

The next morning Corky squatted behind the bushes. He had one of his mother's big white dinner napkins to wave. But he had no chance to use it.

"Never you mind," said Skip a little later. "Money is still disappearing. It's happened in the fifth-grade room and in the eighth-grade room . . . We'll catch him yet, I know we will!"

"It might not be a 'him'," said Nogs thoughtfully. "It could be a girl, you know."

"Corky," said Skip, changing the subject. "Could I stay after school and practice holding Sam for a few minutes? I—I mean, I'm gonna have to get used to him sometime, before our club initiation night."

Corky looked at him. "I've got to run as soon as the bell rings—I've got a dentist appointment. Oh—all right, Skip, here's the key. You be sure you *lock that cage*, though!"

"And don't let anybody mistake you for the thief!" laughed Jim.

In the morning it was Skip's turn to hide and spy. Corky walked by the bushes to check but he wasn't really expecting anything to happen.

A low whistle made him jump.

"Cork-ee! Shhhhh!" Skip motioned him to get down on his knees.

Corky crawled in behind the bushes. The look in Skip's eyes showed that something was up.

"Watch!" whispered Skip.

Corky rested his field glasses against the windowsill and took a long look.

"But the room is empty, Skip."

"Here, let me look," ordered Skip. In a minute or two he grabbed Corky's shoulder. "Do you see what I see? He's there!"

Corky grabbed the glasses back. "Why, that's Mr. Baker! The robber! He's going through my desk . . . and now Carla's . . . and Jim's!"

At Jim's desk, Mr. Baker got the shock of his life. So did Corky Downs. He stared through the field glasses and his mouth fell open. Instead of pulling out an envelope of money, the janitor pulled out Sam!

"Yoooooweeeeee!" His scream came right through the windowpane. Skip waved the white flag. Corky leaped through the side door and into the classroom. He had Sam safely in his own hands before the janitor could get away. A minute later, Skip came in.

"So we caught you red-handed!" they bellowed. "Stealing money from kids' desks! Wait until Mr. Mac hears about this!"

They had him cornered. Corky racked his brains trying to think of things to say. He wanted to stall for time. Mr. Baker did not look as if he would try to get by two angry boys with a dangerous-looking snake.

"Sam caught him," chuckled Skip. "I had a hunch yesterday. When I got here today, I saw Mr. Baker working around the other side of the building. So—I already had the key to Sam's cage in my pocket—I tiptoed in and put Sam into Jim's desk. Just in case. Corky, you aren't sore, are you?"

"No," said Corky. "The desks have a crack where the hinge is, so Sam got enough air."

Mr. Baker was looking from the snake to the classroom door.

"I hear a siren," said Skip with a sigh of relief. "The police are here."

"Well, well!" exclaimed Miss Puckett when she heard the news.

"Tsk!" said Miss White. "I never did like the way that man mopped the floor in my Home Ec room. He left sticky spots."

Mr. Mac stopped by the room to congratulate the boys. "I've asked that this be kept out of the papers, fellows," he told them. "I feel sorry for a man like Baker. A news article would make it harder for him to get another job. You don't mind, do you? You're famous enough anyway around here, with your houseboat adventures and your snake. You don't need any extra publicity!"

"We don't mind," they said all at once.

Corky took a deep breath. Now Mom and Dad wouldn't find out that Sam was at school!

"That snake is the real hero of the day," declared Mr. Mac. He went off chuckling. At three thirty, he waited for Corky and handed him a small carton. The note on it said "For the hero." When Corky opened it up, he found two fat mice, which Detective Sam devoured in a hurry.

"Let's pool our money and take Pauline some ice cream to celebrate," said Jim. "She helped in this capture too."

"You said it!" agreed Corky. "We couldn't have done it without Skip . . . and Pauline . . . and Sam!"

CHAPTER 13

A QUEER DAY FOR VISITORS

January was over. February whizzed by. "If I'm going to plan a History of Reptiles exhibit, I'd better get to work," said Corky to the other D.C.s one day. "Lots of kids have already started their art and science projects for the May Open House."

For days and days he made lists on scraps of paper. He would need diagrams and photographs and drawings. There would be a big map of the world. He would mark the few countries like Antarctica and Ireland that have no snakes.

He was keeping a list of the myths about snakes that are not true, and another list of the ways snakes are helpful to mankind.

Most of his drawings were hidden away, but one day Mom saw him looking through an old *Natural History* magazine for pictures of venomous reptiles. "Oh, Corky," she said. "Snakes again?"

"Don't you *ever* get reptiles out of your head, son?"

asked his father. "Have you used your new bird glasses once?"

"Certainly! Use 'em every day, just about." It was the truth, wasn't it? He'd used those binoculars to find snakes, to catch thieves, to search for footprints. . .

"I don't know why I like snakes better than birds, Dad. All I know is that I want to be a herpetologist."

"A *what?*" asked his parents in one breath.

"A herpetologist. A scientist who specializes in the study of reptiles. I'll go to college if I have to, to be one."

"That's a long way off. You've time to change your mind." But Mr. Downs looked at his redheaded son with a curious gleam in his eye.

Corky did his drawings at his desk table in his bedroom, but he kept them stored in a box in the D.C. shack. They were pretty good drawings, especially the one of the cobra ready to strike.

"You're a real artist," said Skip one afternoon when he was looking at the latest addition to the stack of sketches.

"I didn't know I could do it. It's fun," said Corky.

February was a time for trips.

"Field trips help to combat the midwinter slump," the children heard Mr. Mac say to a teacher. "Lessen the chance of truancy."

"What's he talking about?" asked Nogs. "I haven't wanted to cut school for ages. I'm afraid I'll miss something."

There were trips to factories and shipyards, trips to a sawmill, a fish hatchery, and a tree farm. Nobody got to go on all of them, but each boy or girl went about once a week.

In February the Grow group began to get ready for spring. Some weeks rain poured down without stopping. But sometimes there were three or four days when the river looked like a silver fish caught in a net of sunshine. The air was so balmy that the boys could work outside in their shirt sleeves.

Seed packets had to be sorted. One company had donated thousands of envelopes of seeds, both flower and vegetable. The flats for the greenhouse had to be finished. The ground that was to be farmed had to be made ready. On clear days, the boys dug and raked and helped Mr. Fairly haul loads of manure from a nearby farm.

The base of the new greenhouse was a slab of concrete. Once it had been a tennis court. The boys learned how to mix and pour concrete. They filled every dip and crack of the old slab. They put a new edge around it, with holes where the greenhouse struts would fit.

"If it doesn't rain," said Mr. Fairly early in March, "we'll have that greenhouse up before the week is out. It will take only one day if you fellows can get here at seven thirty."

"Tomorrow!" shouted several voices.

"Tomorrow it shall be! Why not?"

"I'll spend the night with you, Corky," decided Nogs. He was now quite at home in the Downs household and often spent the night. His extra pair of pajamas was folded in Corky's bottom drawer.

"Wear old clothes if the sun is shining. Set your alarms.

Don't bother with lunch money. Miss White's Home Ec girls have promised us a picnic, as long as I let them know the night before," announced Mr. Fairly.

When the alarm went off at six thirty, both Corky and Nogs lay in the big bed with their eyes squinched shut.

"I don't *hear* rain," said Nogs. Warily, he opened an eye. "Yippee! It's clear! Get up, Corky, let's go!"

"Lucky bums," said Pauline, catching up to them on the way to school. She had been back for over a week, no crutches, no limp. She had kept up with her work at home, so she was not having a hard time. But she would rather be out putting up the greenhouse than sitting inside at a desk.

"You get to cook our lunch," Corky said. "And every kid in the school is going to help plant seeds."

The Grow boys helped Mr. Fairly lift every one of the greenhouse arches over to the side door of the shop.

"Now, one by one, we'll carry them out and set them on the grass near the concrete slab. Mike, Roy, Jim—you get on the far end. When I say go, get ready to lift again. One . . . two . . . three!"

Partway through the door they got stuck.

"Twist to the left! More! O.K., now a little more!"

"Push!" called one boy.

"Pull!" suggested another.

Mr. Fairly stood at the front, doing his best to get the widest part of the arch in a position where it could be shoved through the door. Beads of sweat stood out on his forehead. At last he raised a brawny arm. "Halt!"

Everyone had a different idea. Everyone talked at once. When he had quieted the boys, the teacher said, "*These arches are not going to fit through the door of the shop."*

The one thing nobody had remembered to do when the arches were being built was to plan a way to get them out of the building!

With much pulling and pushing, the first arch was worked back out of the doorway. When at last it was leaning safely against the wall of the shop again, Mr. Fairly wiped his forehead with his handkerchief. He smiled. "It's a kind of joke!" he said.

"Do we have to take them apart to get them out?" asked Mike.

"How about taking off the door?" This was Skip's idea. "It would give us an extra inch or so."

"We are going to need more room than that."

"The double door over there, leading into the hall, is wide enough!" said Corky. He had been going around and around the shop, thinking. "Can't we get them out of the shop room that way, and then lift them through one of those big front windows upstairs?"

"I believe we could!" declared Mr. Fairly. "One of you please find Noah and help him bring a ladder. We'll have to remove the window frames first, but that isn't any problem." He smiled broadly. "It might be a good idea to measure the window first, so we don't do all this work for nothing."

"May I help?" The principal was standing in the hall, jacket and tie off, shirt sleeves rolled over his elbows. He enjoyed taking part in school projects. He had worked hard on one of the big arches.

By noon, the frame was out of the front window of the school. All but two arches had been carried outside. Some were being put up over the concrete slab in the meadow. Others were lying on the school lawn. So was the great roll of plastic that would cover the outside of the greenhouse, and the chicken wire that would help to hold everything in place.

Nobody wanted to stop for lunch. The boys had just begun to argue with Mr. Fairly about it when along came a girl from Miss White's room. She handed a note to the Shop instructor.

"Miss White's girls are ready to bring on the deviled eggs, carrot sticks, tuna-fish sandwiches, potato chips, and baked beans for anyone who *is* hungry. Those who do not wish to eat may sit on the grass and rest."

Many appetites came back in a hurry.

Corky got permission to go in and get Sam. "He likes the sun, Mr. Fairly. I promise I won't let him out of my hands. He'll stay around my neck. I know he will."

"Very well," said the Shop instructor. After a long, hard morning, he did not care whether a snake came to the picnic or not.

"Someday," said Fred, leaning over to rub Sam along the back, "you should write a book, Corky. About the adventures of Sam. Gee, he's been in a shipwreck, and caught a robber, and everything!"

"I might," said Corky, "or I might not." He added nonchalantly, "I may not have time if I'm off hunting for specimens in the Congo or Brazil."

"Does it take long to get used to holding him?" asked one boy, wide-eyed at the way Corky's pet lolled around his owner's neck.

"Shucks!" jeered Nogs. "Anyone can do it. Look at me!"

Before Corky could tell Nogs about the promise to Mr. Fairly, Nogs grabbed Sam and stuck him around his own neck.

"Look!" he cried as Sam settled himself comfortably on a new neck. "Up there! Kites!"

He pointed to four kites flying high above them in the sky.

"They must be part of Miss Puckett's science experiment," said Skip. "The kids in the class were tying postcards onto their kites so that whoever found them could mail them back. Sort of like what we did with the messages in bottles. Only we never did get any answers."

"There's another! And another!" shouted Fred.

"I see five more!" cried another boy, pointing the other way.

Everyone watched eagerly. Some of the kites had gone so high that they were only specks in the sky.

"I've counted nineteen," said Skip at last. "All on their way someplace."

"Twenty," corrected a woman's voice. "But this one has reached its destination."

"Lucy Puckett! What are you doing in that tree?" roared Mr. Fairly.

Mr. Mac, who had come to the picnic too, hurried over to the tall tree near the road. Perched like a small bird on a very high branch was Miss Puckett.

"I've snagged my good brown sweater and put a run in my stockings," she said, "but I can't seem to reach this silly thing." She pointed to a canary-colored kite tangled in a branch above her.

"Don't go any farther! I'll find a ladder. Has anyone seen

Noah?" Mr. Mac strode off.

"Please, Miss Puckett, do *not* climb higher than that," begged Mr. Fairly. He and the Grow students gathered at the base of the tree. They craned their necks to talk to Lucy Puckett.

"I am very light," she said. Carefully she began to climb. She disappeared into a green web of leaves.

"Say, boys!" she called, now completely out of sight. "I've found the most wonderful nest! Oh, dear!"

"What in the dickens has happened?" hollered Mr. Fairly.

"I've scared the mother robin away from the nest."

There was a slight cracking sound. "Don't worry. I'm safe. But the branch I was on snapped," Miss Puckett reported. "I'm afraid it was the only one I could reach to get down. My legs are too short to touch the one below it."

"I'm the lightest one. I'll go up and see if I can help!" While everyone watched, astonished, Nogs shinnied up the tree.

"Come back here this minute!" commanded Mr. Fairly.

"Nogs!" shouted Corky, too late. "You've got Sam!"

"Oh, so I do!" exclaimed Nogs when he stopped to rest on a branch. "He'll be all right. And I will too. Don't get upset, Mr. Fairly. Whoops!"

Hastily, he straddled another branch. "Gee, this tree is full of dead limbs! That one cracked too. Now I guess I'm stuck along with Miss Puckett. Yoo-hoo! Miss Puckett, can you see me?"

"This is too ridiculous for words!" said Mr. Fairly.

Mr. Mac had returned. "I forgot that Noah has the key

to the storeroom where we keep the longest ladder, and I can't find him."

"That one we used this morning is much too short anyway," Mr. Fairly told him. "Mr. Mac, you'll have to call the fire department."

"I can reach the kite from here," called Miss Puckett. She was trying to cheer them up. "I've just got to undo a few knots."

"And I've got tight hold of Sam," said Nogs. "You can put this in your book, Corky."

"Let's get back on our job, boys," ordered their teacher.

"Aw, Mr. Fairly!"

"Can't we wait to see the fire truck?"

"We've lost an hour or more," began the teacher.

"Here's the fire truck now," said someone.

The firemen arrived with a ladder truck. Behind the red engine was a station wagon loaded with people. It stopped at the school. Some men and women got out. They stared at the mob of children on the front lawn, the teachers, the firemen. They looked at the large windowpanes propped against the shrubbery, and the giant arches that had not yet been carried to the meadow.

"Has there been an explosion?" asked a lady in a flowered hat.

"For the love of Mike, what's going on?" exclaimed a man. He went over and strained to look into the tree, to see what everyone was so excited about.

Corky found his tongue. "The principal and Mr. Fairly are explaining everything to the firemen. A kite got stuck in the tree when we were putting up our greenhouse. Oh,

first the greenhouse arches got stuck in the shop and we had to take out a window . . ." He waved toward the window frames. "Then Miss Puckett got stuck in the tree while she was getting the kite, and after that—"

"I got stuck too," chimed in Nogs. Unnoticed, he had found a way to get to the ground without assistance. Sam was still around his neck. "It's a sticky day. Can we help you?"

"Maybe you can," said the man. He cast a nervous glance at Sam. "We are a group of parents who felt it might be interesting to spend an afternoon here at school. We—ah—we thought we'd pick any normal day instead of making an appointment. We have heard so much about this Grow Program."

"This is not a normal day," Corky explained.

"It is too!" said Nogs. "Just as normal as any other day. There's always something interesting going on. Snakes getting loose, burglars . . ." Corky silenced him with a sharp look.

"Go right on in and look around," he told the man.

"Flying kites during school!" exclaimed another parent. "Think of that!"

"Yes, think of that!" snapped Lucy Puckett from the tree. "It was a class experiment concerning wind directions. Benjamin Franklin experimented with a kite in his studies, and we are merely following his example."

Within an hour, she was on solid ground. The kite had been properly launched. The parents were on a tour of the school with Mr. Mac, and the greenhouse was going up.

The boys stayed until the job was finished. It was exciting to see the greenhouse that they had planned and built with their own hands. They would start using it tomorrow!

It was five thirty. Mr. Fairly treated everyone to a round of Coca-Cola. Corky was dog-tired when he went home.

"You must have had quite a day!" called his mother. "Better clean up for dinner. Did you spend the whole day getting that greenhouse up?"

"Not quite," said Corky. He stared out the bathroom window at the cherry tree. Pretty soon he tiptoed out the back door. Sure enough, there, caught among the blossoms, was a canary-colored kite!

CHAPTER 14

FOUND OUT

April came.

A pair of house finches built a nest in the tree outside Corky's window. Early each morning before it was time to get up for school, he lay in bed and watched them. He proved, thereby, that he did use his binoculars for birds. His father, knocking on the door to wake him, was pleased.

There was so much to do inside the greenhouse and out in the meadow. Grow students planted new shrubs and flowers around the school too.

School days were so busy that Corky found he must work on his reptile history project after hours. The best place to do it was in the peace and quiet of the shack. The D.C.s had their club meetings twice a week. Sometimes one or two of them kept Corky company on other days, but most of the time he was alone. Pauline had taken up marbles since the doctor said no skateboard until summer. Jim and Skip had baseball practice. Nogs had to catch the school bus, since Bill did not want him to ride his bike in afternoon traffic.

Sometimes Corky felt like a real scientist doing research. One day maybe he *would* discover an important fact, something no one else in the world knew about reptiles!

He wanted his project to be good. He had been able to buy three back issues of the *Natural History* magazine and two of another nature magazine with colored photographs of Gila monsters and desert lizards.

Miss Puckett lent him still another magazine from a zoo in the East. He could not cut pictures out of this, so he ended up having to draw the iguanas.

The last chart was to be a giant sheet of white poster board. When Corky laid his pictures out on it, he found he needed a few that he had not been able to find in any book or magazine.

The Reptile House at the zoo! Maybe Bob Elton could help! For two Saturdays in a row, Corky went by bus to the zoo. Bob held the nonpoisonous snakes so Corky could get a close look at their markings.

He took a fifteen-minute "coffee break" and walked Corky back to the bus stop, talking all the while about reptiles. "Keep up the good work, man!" he said when they parted. He wrote down the date of the Open House at school and promised to come.

On Sunday afternoon, Corky took his new drawings over to the shack. He stood outside, trying to decide if he was awake or in a dream.

The door was locked. Skip must have left the window open to air the place out. He had been planning to finish the inside paint job, Corky remembered.

Nothing wrong with airing out the shack. But there, in front of him, were footprints! They led right up to the open window! There were more prints going off into the bushes.

"Well, I'll be a monkey's uncle!" whispered Corky. He stooped to look at the prints. They might have been made by a girl's tennis shoes.

Corky walked around the outside of the shack, searching for more prints. He didn't find any footprints, but he did pick up a child's toy, a miniature truck.

Was the stranger friend or foe? Was she the person who belonged to the singing voice in the woods? What about the man's boot prints they had found?

There were no boot prints today.

Would his drawings be safe inside the shack? Corky felt uneasy.

He unlocked the door and went in. The place smelled of fresh paint. Skip had done a neat job. Nothing had been moved. His pets were safe. He checked them all. Hopper, his toad, sat on a rock in his cage, sunning himself. Toby, the tiny lizard, was safe. The garter snakes were in their box.

Skip must be starting to like snakes! He had found some small earthworms and put them in the cage.

Corky decided it would be safe to leave his drawings. At least until tomorrow. He put the new ones on top of the stack and weighted them with a rock. Then he tore home, got his bike out of the garage, and rode down to the marina to find Jim.

Jim was fishing over the side of his houseboat. "I've got an extra line," he called when Corky came down the ramp. "What's new with you?"

"What's new!" exploded Corky. "Wait till you *hear* what's new!" Quickly he told his news. "Let's hustle, Jim!

They looked like very fresh prints. Maybe we can find out who made them."

"Maybe we don't want to find out," said Jim. He reeled in his line. "If it's the owner of the shack . . . well, maybe it's no more D.C. clubhouse!"

He lifted his bike from the porch of the houseboat to the floating walk. Corky helped him wheel it along the walk and up the steep ramp to the parking lot. They sped over to the shack.

When they reached the wooded lot, both of them clapped their hands over their mouths.

"More prints!" yelled Corky. "Those weren't there before, and I've been gone only fifteen minutes!"

Corky unlocked the door and went in and got the little truck. "It's funny I didn't see any child's shoe prints."

"It's stickery out there where we haven't cleared it," said Jim. "Whoever was here might have carried a little boy. Say, didn't Skip do a keen job with the paint!"

They both fell silent, thinking. After all this work, they might have to find another place to hold D.C. meetings.

"Tomorrow," said Corky, "I'm going to bring Sam's cage over on my skateboard. Will you help, Jim? He's good at scaring people away!"

As soon as they heard the news, Skip and Nogs and Pauline rushed over to see the prints.

"Must have been after I went there yesterday," said Skip. "Around two o'clock I checked the paint and gave your snakes some worms. I didn't see a single footprint. That's when I left the window open to air out."

"Thanks for feeding the snakes," Corky said. "I didn't go over until nearly four, and the prints were there."

"What will we tell Miss Puckett if we take Sam?"

"Let her think we're lending him to someone," said Jim. "She doesn't have to know we're lending him to ourselves!"

"We can use my skateboard," Pauline offered. "My house is closer than yours. We won't want to waste any time."

After school they sat on the front steps waiting for her to get back. She seemed to be gone a long time. At last she appeared with the skateboard under her arm. She giggled. "Mother saw me, and, boy, was she hopping mad! I told her I wasn't going to break my promise to the doctor, but I needed the board for something else. She kept wanting to know what for. I couldn't think of a thing to say! I ended up telling her the truth—that we were carting your snake someplace on it. She laughed. She think's Sam is beautiful!"

"I wish my mom did!" Corky sighed. "Let's go."

They wheeled the heavy cage to the riverfront and took turns carrying it, two by two, from the road to the shack.

"We can leave him outside while we have our meeting," puffed Corky. "I'll take out his flowerpot so he won't curl up and go to sleep. He can be our watchman."

Sam's box was placed squarely in front of the door.

"Oh, Skip, it's pretty!" squealed Pauline when she saw the paint job. Skip had followed his plan. Every wall of the shack was a different color—one red, one white, one green, and one black.

Corky took a box of thumbtacks from his pocket. He began to pin up his best drawings on the white wall. "This place is neat! It looks like a regular science lab!"

It did, too. At the end of the long shelf was Jim Mahony's microscope, bought with savings from his newspaper route.

Beside it was a cigar box of glass slides. Skip had brought a large magnifying glass. Pauline had donated two paperback books on wild flowers. On the shelf, too, were all the animal cages. There was a box of shells and a box of rocks and minerals. There were the bird nests and fossils, and an enormous chunk of petrified wood. Pauline claimed her mother would never miss it as a doorstop.

Jim passed around a box of crackers. He offered the rest of the D.C.s drinks of water from his army canteen. "We don't want anybody to get in here and ruin our stuff," he said while they munched.

"Heck, no!" cried Corky. "All my good pictures!"

"But what can we do?" asked Pauline and Nogs. "We don't own the land this shack is on. If somebody wants it to store garden tools or a boat or something, we'll have to give it back."

"Stupid!" chuckled Corky. "There isn't any place to make a garden unless the brush is cleared away first. And a boat wouldn't fit through the door."

"Well, well, well!" boomed a hearty voice outside. "If it isn't Sam? How on earth did *you* get here?"

For one second, the D.C.s couldn't move.

"That's the principal!" shouted Corky. "Mr. Mac, it's *us!*"

The principal crouched, entered the shack, and folded his long body onto the small chair the D.C.s offered him.

"The mystery is solved!" he declared.

"*Our* mystery?" They stared, baffled.

"*My* mystery. The one I've been working on for months. This piece of property has been in my family for many years, but it has not been used since the early part of the century. There was a house once, but it burned down. I'm sure blackberry brambles and shrubs have long since covered up the remains. Nobody bothered to do anything with this old tool shed. Then, suddenly, one day when I wandered by, what did I see? A padlock on the door and a new windowpane! I've been watching the place ever since." He waved toward the curtains Pauline had hung at the window. "Rather hard to spy when those things are drawn."

Corky was looking at the principal's feet. He had on his after-school slacks and a pair of hiking boots! "We saw your footprints," he said to Mr. Mac. "We thought *we* were spying on *you!*"

Everyone burst out laughing.

"But," said Skip, "we did hear a girl singing. And Corky found a toy truck. You don't have a baby boy. There must have been someone else."

Mr. Mac grinned. "You may have heard my daughter. She likes to take her little boy—my grandson Jimmy—on long walks. They go almost every day, rain or shine. She sometimes short-cuts through here. In fact, it was my daughter, Jane, who peeked through the open window yesterday and discovered the fresh paint job."

A smile flickered across his face. "You children kept us guessing. My wife thought we ought to call the police. But Jane and I felt that anyone who was kind enough to fix a place up so nicely didn't need a policeman on his trail."

Corky had been deep in thought. Suddenly he said, "Mr. Mac, what now? I mean, we'd like to keep on using your shack. But, of course, if you wanted to turn it back into a— a tool shed or something . . ."

"Use it!" said Mr. Mac. "And welcome! Someday in the future when my daughter and her husband have saved

152

enough money, they have plans to build on this property. I've deeded it over to them. But"—his eyes twinkled—"I doubt if that happens before you youngsters are through with high school."

"Whoopee!" shouted Nogs and Jim and Corky and Skip and Pauline. "You mean it? Oh, boy! Oh, boy!"

"Of course," Mr. Mac went on, "no one need be the wiser if you wish to keep it a secret. I do feel it might be nice to let your families see what a fine job you've done." His eyes traveled to the shelves of treasures, and Corky's drawings on the wall.

"Who did those pictures?"

"Corky," said everyone else.

"Corky Downs!" exclaimed the principal. And then, again, "Corky Downs! You never cease to amaze me." He looked as if he wished to say something more, but changed his mind.

"Mr. Mac," said Corky slowly, "we'd like to keep our clubhouse a secret for a while. My folks don't know I still have Sam. They think I've given him away, along with most of my other pets. I haven't exactly lied, because they never really asked. I—I've been trying to find a way to let them know . . ."

"A secret it shall be then," agreed Mr. Mac. "You can bank on me."

He stayed long enough to admire the nests and to look through every one of Corky's diagrams and drawings.

"Keep the state science fair in mind," he told Corky. "Judges go around to the various school exhibits and open houses. They select the projects they think are best. Your reptile history is excellent, Corky. Excellent!"

"Wow!" breathed Skip when he had left. "That's over! No more mystery!"

"How about that?" asked Pauline. "All of us spying on each other!"

"Come help me lug Sam's cage inside," said Corky. "Tomorrow we can take him back to school. He's done his job." He removed the key to the cage from around his neck and unlocked the little padlock. "Listen, Sam," he said to his pet, "you've brought me good luck all year long! You're the greatest!"

CHAPTER 15

CARNIVAL

"Ouch! Ouch! Ouch! I guess I never will like sewing!" Pauline was sitting cross-legged on the floor of the D.C. shack, trying to put the hem in an apron. "It's lopsided," she said, holding it up for them to see. "Oh, dear, I'll have to start over again."

"You should see the things *we've* made to sell at Carnival," boasted Corky. "Game boards, footstools, spice shelves, napkin holders, letter boxes, lamps, bird feeders—"

"And, gee whiz, the greenhouse tables are full of the stuff we're getting ready—marigolds, pansies, geraniums . . . ," Nogs took up the chant where Corky left off.

"The best fun is going to be the cakewalk," said Jim.

Skip shook his head. "Not for me. I'll take the pie-throwing contest. Carla says the girls have baked and frozen stacks and stacks of custard pies."

"Are they gonna *waste* all that good pie?" Nogs looked shocked.

Carnival was a few weeks away. There was no time to

hike or ride bikes or skateboard. No time to fish or go hunting for baby frogs in the slough behind the school meadow. No time for regular D.C. meetings, either.

All through the warm, sunny days of May, the boys and girls worked. They were beginning to build the Carnival booths. In order to get them finished in time, many of the boys stayed after school to help.

Each night Corky arrived home with his shoes caked with mud, his face grimy, and his hands blistered. Dad would give him a queer look. Probably he was wondering what was going on over at the River School!

"He doesn't talk about it anymore," Corky said to Nogs. "But I get a shiver in my backbone when he looks at me that way. I'm sure he's thinking about next year. I hope I don't have to transfer to a different school! And say, Nogs, I've got to figure out something to do with Sam this summer. I mean during the weeks we're all busy taking trips or going to Y camp."

Things began to get more complicated toward the end of May. Miss Puckett promised that the trip to eastern Oregon might be as long as ten days if . . . if the sixth-graders could earn as much as seventy-five dollars at the Carnival. And if she could find a willing parent to help chaperon and drive the school bus.

Uncle Dick wrote to ask if Corky would like to work on his ranch in Washington for the month of August.

"It's the chance of a lifetime!" exclaimed Mr. Downs. "Write him tonight, Corky, and let him know how pleased you are."

"I don't want to," said Corky.

"What?" His dad found this hard to believe. "Eastern Washington is like the wheat country of Oregon. The country you love . . . space . . . sky . . ."

"But I *like* Portland," Corky almost shouted. "I didn't at first, but I do now! I don't want to go anyplace else for the summer. Except on Miss Puckett's field trip."

Underneath the excitement of getting ready for Carnival and Open House, he felt a little blue.

"This is the first time in my whole life," he told Nogs, "that I've ever been sorry to see summer vacation come."

"Not me," said Nogs. "Bill says I can spend a week on Mahonys' houseboat. And we're looking for a better house to live in. And, Corky, Bill says if we let him come along, we can camp out overnight in the shack anytime we want to!"

"You told him?" asked Corky.

"Sure. He won't come snooping around."

What would Mom and Dad say if they heard about the D.C. clubhouse? The camp-out idea was great. But in order to get permission, he'd have to tell them about the shack.

"I'm going to wait to tell my folks until after Carnival," he said.

He had finished every drawing for the History of Reptiles. He had collected the things he wanted to display. One of the very best things, the D.C.s agreed, was the live mother garter snake with her thirty-one squiggling, wriggling babies.

Corky had come upon her den on a bike hike with Nogs and Pauline. "Not all snakes bear live young," he told the others. He took his lunch out of the shoe box and carried

158

his new find back to the clubhouse. It was Pauline who
nursed the baby snakes along with bits of flaked fish and
earthworms.

"How come you're the one who finds the good stuff,
Corky?" asked Jim.

Corky shrugged. "Maybe I look harder."

Carnival night came at last. Bill and Nogs had dinner at
the Downs home. It was a nice night, so they walked to
school instead of driving.

Corky watched Mom and Dad start looking at the exhibits. It would be a long time before they got down to the
end of the hall where History of Reptiles was on display.
He went off to find his friends.

He was full of dinner, but the sight of food made him
hungry all over again. He squandered four nickels on popcorn balls and some double-Dutch fudge. The label on the
package of fudge told that it had been made by none other
than Pauline Tyler. She was busy selling cookies. When
she had taken care of her customers, she greeted Corky.

"Hi, Corky. How do you like my candy?"

"Poison," he joked, pretending to keel over. "No, really,
Pauline, it's good." He crammed the last two pieces into
his pocket and wandered over to the balloon dart game.

"I hit seven!" shouted Jim. "Bang!"

Corky's record was five. He won a sailor hat and cocked
it rakishly over one eye. Just then Nogs came up. "Nobody
can guess who is behind the sheet in the pie-throwing contest. I think the man might be Mr. Henry."

Corky followed him to the other end of the gym. He

bought three pies. He aimed with care at the faces peeking through the holes.

"Yeo, heave ho!" called a voice from behind the sheet.

"That isn't Mr. Henry, it's Mr. Fairly!" Corky's custard pie hit him—squoosh in the eye!

Skip was throwing pies too. "I think the other one is Miss White," he chuckled as he aimed. "I saw a teeny bit of blond hair when she moved. Isn't it funny? We're clobbering her with the pies baked by her own class!"

Bill Noggins came by. He treated each boy to another round of pies and bought some for himself.

"Corky," he said. "That reptile history exhibit is the best thing in the whole show. Lots of parents are down there looking at it. Oh, by the way, someone wanted to see you. A tall fellow about my age, with glasses."

"Bob Elton!" exclaimed Corky. He dashed out of the gym to find Bob. His friend was not in front of the display. But Mom and Dad were. They were talking to Mr. Mac so seriously that they did not see Corky coming.

"The boy has real talent," Mr. Mac was saying. "Maybe he can't spell Mississippi or Bunker Hill. But he doesn't make a mistake when it comes to 'reticulated python.' My stars! You should see the reptile encyclopedia that son of yours has been using."

He turned and saw Corky. "I've been boasting about the work you've done this year, Corky."

"If this exhibit is any example," said Mr. Downs quietly, "I agree. It is a fine display, Corky. I never realized you could draw like that!"

"I just found out myself, Dad."

Mom started to say something, but she stopped and gave Corky a little squeeze instead.

Mr. Mac pumped his hand. "The judges have been by, Corky. Your exhibit will be going to the state science fair. That's quite an honor!"

Corky wanted to jump and yell. He wanted to holler, "Whoopee!" His freckled face became scarlet. When he tried to talk, no words came out.

"Your friend, Mr. Elton, had to leave to catch a train," said Dad. "But we had time for a brief chat. Corky, I think you have something with this herpetology stuff. Looks to me like it's grown into a serious interest instead of a here-today-and-gone-tomorrow hobby."

"We've discovered where Sam has been spending the year," laughed Mom. "Son, since he is partly responsible for the honor you won, don't you think it is high time to bring him home?"

This time Corky did jump and whoop and holler. "Gee, Mom! Gee, Dad! Thanks! Yoweeee!" He tore down the hall to tell his friends the good news. Halfway down, he skidded to a stop and backtracked.

"What made you change your mind?" he asked.

His mother smiled. "I got talking to Mrs. Mahony and Mrs. Tyler. If they aren't afraid of him, I guess I can get over my feelings. And I'm so proud of you that I want to show it in some way."

"This is the best way!" Corky flung his arms around his mother so hard that he nearly knocked her off her feet. Then he tore off to find Nogs.

The rest of the Carnival was like a dream. There were relay races with parents lined up against their children. There was an auction of silly objects.

Mr. Henry bid five dollars for a large cat-shaped cushion. "It's for Danny, my St. Bernard," he announced. Pretty little Miss White, with a trace of custard pie on her cheek, surprised everyone by bidding high for an inlaid board and a set of chessmen.

"She's a fiend when it comes to chess," whispered Mr. Mac, who was standing near Corky and Nogs. "You boys should challenge her to a game!"

Mr. Mahony bid for the mystery package. He opened it and found a blond wig. Amid roars of laughter and much hand clapping, he put it on and did a curtsy.

Corky laughed and clapped, but his mind was on Sam and the honor he had won. In a daze, he followed the crowd into the cafeteria. There the Carnival ended with a funny musical fashion show put on by the school staff.

"Mr. Mac in an old-fashioned bathing suit and black stockings! Ho, ho, ho!" howled Nogs. He punched Corky. "Hey, Cork, look! That's Miss Puckett in the moustache and striped vest and straw hat! And get a load of Noah in a wig and high-button shoes!"

As soon as the musical was over, Miss Puckett hurried down into the audience to find Corky. "Benjamin, I'm proud of that exhibit! I wish my father were here to see it. He has thoroughly enjoyed my letters about the adventures of Sam!"

"Thank you," said Corky. "Oh, Miss Puckett, my parents say it's all right if Sam comes home again! May I get him now?"

Bill went home to his house, but Nogs was spending the night with Corky. It was warm outside. The popcorn balls and the fudge had made them both thirsty. They sat out on the back steps drinking ginger ale and trying to see who could spot a satellite first.

"Parents!" said Corky slurping down another gulp of ginger ale. "Sometimes they're nutty. But nice."

"How do you mean?" asked Nogs. He scanned the sky for a satellite. "How do you mean, nutty? I think your folks are great, Corky!"

"Me too. But—well—take Dad. First he seems so far away it doesn't feel as if he's my father anymore. He's been so busy I thought we'd never go camping or fishing again. But tonight he told Miss Puckett he'd try to get his vacation at the right time to be bus driver for our field trip."

"Say!" Nogs picked up a pebble out of the grass and tossed it into the night. "Why didn't we think of asking him before?"

"We didn't think of it," said Corky, "because I had him wrong. I didn't know he was the adventuring type. And imagine my mother *wanting* to have Sam home again!"

"Well, he *is* home," said Nogs. "And she said you can take him out and hold him when your bedroom door is shut. As long as you remember—"

"To lock the cage!" said Corky. "Let's go see him now!"

CHAPTER 16

INITIATION

"This g-g-grass is c-cold! Can't we hurry up and get the running part over with so we can go inside?" begged Nogs.

It was initiation night. The D.C.s had permission to hold the ceremony after dark and to spend the night at the clubhouse.

Mr. and Mrs. Downs had been over to inspect and admire the place. They liked it!

The club members had made up a special ritual. First all members would run barefoot around the shack three times. This was a tough course. Brambles and vines had been cleared away, but there were plenty of gravelly places and a few forgotten sticker bushes.

Off they went like a pack of wild men. The second time around, Pauline fell and banged her knee. Jim Mahony caught his shirttail on a bush. Inside the shack, they collapsed on top of the sleeping bags, breathless.

"Next, we get to drink the *brew* I made up," said Pauline. "Who's first?"

"You!" said Nogs. "Because you're the one that made it."

"Nothing doing! Oh, all right." Pauline poured a thick liquid from a bottle into a measuring cup. She held her nose and swallowed. "Yum!" She rubbed her stomach, pretending it tasted delicious.

"It can't be too bad," whispered Nogs. "Me next." He grabbed the bottle and poured himself a cupful of the stuff.

"Oh, help! Ish!" He grabbed Jim's canteen for a mouthful of water, then leaned out the open window and spit into the bushes.

"It's so dark I can't see," said Jim. Corky held the flashlight so Jim could have his drink. Then Skip, then Corky himself. He took a big swallow to get it over with. "Roooops —phewy! That was horrid! What's in it?"

"Molasses, vinegar, mustard, red-hot pepper, salt, ketchup, and orange pop," said Pauline with a giggle.

"I bet you drank out of a different bottle!" Jim accused her. But Pauline only laughed.

"Now everyone must tell what he's done to fix up the club," Corky ordered. That was easier. Skip had painted the walls. Jim had mended the roof. Pauline had supplied most of the broken furniture and the curtains. Corky had given most of the collection on the nature shelf. Nogs had cleared the brambles away.

"Next, what has each one done to help a creature in distress?" asked Jim. "Pauline first."

"I fed you refreshments almost every time," she said, grinning. She look around the circle of faces. "You didn't say the creature had to be a dumb animal. You're all creatures, aren't you?"

"That will do," said Jim sternly. "This initiation is no

joke. How about you, Corky?"

"I kept Sam safe and out of trouble," said Corky. He sighed. "That was work."

"Skip?"

"I took care of Sam during the holidays," said Skip. "And fed the garter snake when everyone else forgot."

"Nogs?"

Nogs cleared his throat. "I—I let three field mice out of the live-mouse traps," he said. Before Pauline and the boys could jump on him, he added, "Don't be sore! Field mice are pretty little things—such big ears and cute noses!"

Corky groaned. "Sabotage! Never mind, Nogs, Sam's had enough to eat without them."

"Last of all," said Pauline, "we must each hold Sam. While we're doing that, let's make up a club yell."

Not one of the D.C. members was afraid of Sam now. "In fact," said Skip, taking him into his own hands and stroking his silky belly, "I have to admit . . . I *like* the way he feels!"

Everyone made up lines for the yell. They ended up with—

> Hurray for Sam
> The marvelous Corn—
> We're glad a snake
> Like him got born!
>
> Hi ho
> Whoopee
> *Wham*
>   Lollapallooza
>   Pickalopooza
> He's the greatest
> Snake what am!

"We'll try it together," said Jim. "Remember to come in hard on the *wham* by banging on the floor. And, remember, it isn't a song. It's a yell."

"A-one and a-two, and a-three . . . ," counted Corky under his breath. Their voices rang out into the night.

> Hi ho
> Whoopee
> *Wham*
>> Lollapallooza
>> Pickalopooza
> He's the greatest
> Snake what am!

Corky had turned the flashlight off. In the velvet-black night they sat feeling pleased with themselves.

"Listen to the peepers!" said Jim softly.

An owl hooted. Nogs shivered. "Give us a light, Corky. I got a splinter in my hand when I banged on the floor."

Corky rummaged for the flashlight.

"*Hi ho whoopee wham!*" The big voice came from outside the cabin.

They jumped and screeched, knocking one another in the dark.

"May I come in, please?" said the voice at the door. "I've brought orange pop and ice cream."

"Bill!" Nogs threw open the door. "You—you spy!"

Bill laughed. He set down his sleeping bag and other bundles and looked around the shack. "This is some clubhouse! Neat, I'd say!"

It was a long time before the refreshments were all gone and the sleeping bags unrolled. Twice they spread them out and found there was not enough room for six.

"I know how to take care of that," said Bill. "I'll sleep outside. I ought to be a guard, anyhow. I'm not a club member."

He picked up his bag and they switched things around a third time. Everyone fit nicely. Pauline had one end near the wall. Corky had the other end near the museum shelf. He reached out and touched Sam's cage.

"Hi ho!" he whispered sleepily. "Whoopee wham! You're the . . . greatest . . . snake what am! Good night, everybody! Good night, old Sam!"

Biography of Mary Phraner Warren

Mary Phraner Warren was born in Brooklyn, New York, and lived all of her girlhood there. From the time she could read and write, she filled many a school notebook with "scribblings."

During high school years at Packer Collegiate Institute, Brooklyn Heights, Mrs. Warren served on the editorial staff of the school literary magazine and reported the school events to the *Brooklyn Eagle*.

After two years at Mount Holyoke, she attended a writer's conference at the University of Colorado in Boulder. She fell in love with the Rocky Mountains and with university life and transferred, later attaining her B.A. in English. At Union Theological Seminary in New York she earned a master's degree in Christian education. Each summer she found a way to return to the West or the Southwest, once working with Mexican migrant farmers, once at Good Shepherd Mission on the Navaho reservation in Fort Defiance, Arizona.

In her seminary years Mrs. Warren worked as a volunteer at St. Luke's Hospital. Later, working on the pediatric play program, she met a seminary student, Lindsay Warren, whom she married.

When the Warren family settled in Salem, Oregon, Mary Warren renewed her old interest in writing, completing five picture books for Concordia, verses and stories for children's magazines, and books for The Westminster Press.

The Warrens and their seven children live in Portland, Oregon.